To Emily,
 May your love and life
always be a little sweet!

Cara Wade

Sugar
&
Spice

CARA WADE

To Emily,
May your love and life
always be a little sweet.

♡
Cara Wade

This is a work of fiction. Names, characters, places, and incidents are either the product of the author's imagination or are used fictionally, and any semblance to the actual persons, living or dead, businesses, companies, events, or locales is entirely coincidental.

First published September 2018

Copyright © Cara Wade 2018

Cover design by Amanda Walker Design Services

Developmental and copy editing provided by Kendra Gaither at Kendra's Editing and Book Services

For my husband, I'm finally doing what you asked me to do!

CHAPTER ONE

*T*he funeral is over and everyone is still in disbelief that she is gone. She was too young, too healthy to be ripped from our family so soon. Aunt Sheryl was the one constant in my life; I could count on her for everything since my mom passed away during my freshman year in high school. Aunt Sheryl made everyone around her smile, and she had a true talent for making the best baked goods around. I have no idea how I am going to manage this all without her.

Two days after we buried her, I'm sitting in her attorney's office, listening to the reading of the will with her husband, my Uncle Rob.

"Finally, to my darling niece, Kaylan Santine, I give you complete control and ownership of *Little Sweet Shoppe*. She has always been good to me and I know she will do wonders for you. Make me proud and keep her in the family."

"What?" I almost choke on my water, so I place the glass on the table in front of me. "I know nothing of owning a bakery! I don't even know how to bake that well. Why isn't she leaving it to you, Uncle Rob?" I ask, panicking.

1

The attorney hands me the will so I can read it myself. I read it once, twice, three times before handing it back and leaning into the fabric chair. *How could she do this? What was she thinking?* I'm shell-shocked as I sit here, staring straight ahead, before my uncle waves his hands in front of my face.

"Kaylan, are you still with us?" Uncle Rob asks.

"Yeah," I whisper. "Why not leave it with you or sell it? Why leave it to me?" I turn my full attention to Uncle Rob, my eyes pleading for answers.

"You were the only one she trusted with the store that is family. You worked there for many summers throughout high school and college. You know the ropes. When we were putting this will together a few years back, she was adamant that you take control of the shop."

I take a deep breath and slowly exhale, my mind racing, trying to think rationally about this, how to make this work. *There are people who work in the bakery that know the ropes, and I could buy some books on how to do it...*

"Uncle Rob, what if I can't do this?" I look at him, my eyes shimmering with unshed tears.

"Kaylan, your aunt had all the faith in the world you could do this. I'm too old to take on something like this, and she couldn't bear to see it close. She felt the shop was too important to the community and refused to sell it to a chain store. She wanted to be able to keep small businesses around." He reaches forward and places a reassuring hand on my knee. "Please try. If things really start going south, we can look into other options, okay?" he asks, a small smile playing on his lips.

I stay silent for a moment, letting the words sink in. "Okay."

"Great, now that's settled, here are the keys." The attorney drops a set of three keys on a ring into my hand. "She owned an apartment upstairs from the bakery as well. The rent of the apartment is included in the rent for the shop. I need you to sign here." He points to the blank line on the paper.

"She had an apartment?" I look at my uncle and he shrugs.

"News to me, sweetheart."

I sign on the line and gather my belongings to leave the office, Uncle Rob in tow.

"Don't be mad at Sheryl," Uncle Rob says, patting my shoulder.

"I'm not mad at her. I just don't understand her! Baking was her passion. I just worked there because it was a job and she let me eat stuff that wasn't sold at night," I scoff lightly. "What am I gonna do? She has employees and bills and everything else. I mean, did she handle all the finances or did she have someone to do that?"

We walk out into the sunny street and begin making our way toward the parking lot across the street.

"She has someone, a nice guy. His name is Dan. He's been over with his wife and kids for dinner a few times. She also has someone who comes in and helps her bake in the mornings and another girl who helps with the front during the day. How about I take you over there this weekend and you can meet everyone? They are reopening on Saturday. I'll do the introductions, and you can start getting a feel for the place." He smiles, trying to reassure me.

"What about my job? I already have one of those with benefits and everything. I can't uproot my life in the city to move out to the suburbs. What about Kevin?" I feel myself start to panic again thinking through all the changes that are about to happen.

"We'll figure it all out. Now, go home, get some sleep, and I'll see you in a few days, okay?" he asks, pulling me into a tight embrace.

"Yeah, I'll see you in a few days." I hug him back, but I'm not feeling any better about the situation at hand.

Getting into my car, I decide to drive over to the shop to have a look around. I park my car in front of the shop and get out to peer into the window. She wasn't into technology, and the shop relied on people coming in to pick up their orders. She refused to have a website, insisting that it took away too much of the charm.

I press my face against the glass and smile, remembering all the summers of tasting the sweet treats and helping customers as they raved about how amazing everything tasted. Aunt Sheryl has, *had,* a way of resonating with people; she could make a room light up just by being in it. The shop has been closed since the funeral. She was well known in the community, as was evident by the turnout at the wake and funeral.

I look around at the chairs on the small tables, and the drink cooler to the right. Everything is exactly as it was the last time I was here. I close my eyes, picturing the happy customers coming to pick up treats for dessert or for a party. The shop was so full of life, and I can almost hear the bell over the door and Aunt Sheryl's infectious laugh as she filled the cream puffs. Concentrating hard, I can smell the sugar in the air, the sweetness just enough to put a smile on someone's face when they open the door. I ponder going in for a minute to have a look around but think better of it at the last second.

I open my eyes again to see the shop still empty and the lights still off. I groan inwardly as I think about how to run this place. First things first, I have to go home and talk with Kevin.

CHAPTER TWO

*T*he ride back to my apartment isn't terrible, and I can't wait to get inside and pop open the bottle of wine I have on the table. I need it after the bomb that was dropped on me today. I park the car, and when I see Kevin is already home, I smile. He is exactly who I need to see right now. I walk up the stairs to our second-floor apartment and smile tiredly when I see him in the kitchen with two glasses of wine poured and at the ready.

"Babe, you're a Godsend. Thank you," I say as I walk toward him and stand on my toes to place a light kiss on his lips, his day stubble tickling my lips slightly.

"I figured it was going to be a long day, and I wanted to be here for you." He pulls me into a tight embrace, and I inhale his scent.

He smells of cinnamon and leather with a subtle amount of something earthy. I look into his brown eyes and smile before pulling back and reaching for the glass of red wine.

"So, I have something I need to talk to you about." I hesitate, studying his face carefully. He motions with his hand to continue as we move into the living room to sit on the couch. "I'm the new owner of *Little Sweet Shoppe*."

"What do you mean, the new owner?" He furrows his brows in confusion.

"Aunt Sheryl left the store to me." I look down and play with the hem of my shirt, a nervous tick I picked up years ago.

"You have a job and a life here already. She can't expect you to drop everything and go play baker, can she?" His voice is soft, but he still sounds confused.

"That's what it seems is going to happen for a while. Uncle Rob wants me to try for a few months, and if it's not working, I can sell it."

"Why didn't she leave it to your uncle? He's her husband, after all." His voice raises slightly in anger or annoyance; I'm having a difficult time distinguishing.

"Why are you getting so upset over this?" I ask, my tone a bit harsher than I mean. "I'm the one who's going to have to move my life out there for a while. I still have to talk to my job, find out if I can work remotely and what that means for me. I have to figure out how the hell I'm going to run a bakery and manage a business." I'm pissed now, the anger rolling off me in waves.

He runs his fingers through his light brown locks and then brings his hand to his face and scrubs his features, groaning in annoyance. "That's not what I meant. That's not how I meant it, Kaylan. I'm sorry." He reaches out and runs the back of his fingers down the side of my cheek tenderly. "This is just insane and I'm freaking out a little. It's going to be fine though, babe; we'll figure it out together." A smile tugs at the corners of his lips and he leans over to kiss my cheek. "When are you going to tell your job?"

"I'm sorry, too. I'm just a little stressed out right now. I don't know when I'll tell them; sooner the better, right?" I take another sip of wine and try to make my brain shut down for a few minutes. I feel like I am going to explode if I can't slow down.

I stand and walk to my purse to gather my phone and call my boss. She is going to freak out, and I hope I'll still have a job. I search through my contacts and land on Karen's name. Pressing the call button, I hold my breath.

"Hi, Kaylan. How's everything going?"

"Hey, Karen. Things are okay." I take a deep breath and continue. "So, my aunt seems to have a real sense of humor about her, and she gave me her bakery."

"What do you mean, *gave* you?"

"I mean, I've been entrusted to own and run the bakery. So," I pause, "I wondered if it would be possible to do some remote work for a few months?"

She sighs heavily. "I'm not sure, Kaylan. I mean, you're one of the best people we have and I don't want to lose you. I need to talk with the others and see if it's something we can arrange for you. How long are you thinking?"

"My uncle wants me to run it for a few months, and if things aren't looking good, then we can look into selling it. I'm still not sure why she didn't leave it with him, but he refuses to take it, too."

"Okay, I'll discuss it with the team tomorrow, and I'll give you a call. When were you planning on taking over the shop?"

"My uncle said the shop is opening again on Saturday, and he is bringing me by then. I imagine he wants me to be there sooner than later."

"Okay. I'm sorry again for your loss though. I know how tough it is," she says, her voice soft with concern.

"Yeah, thanks. I'll talk to you tomorrow, Karen."

I hang up the call and feel the beginning stages of a headache forming. I just want to make all this go away and return to my normal, uneventful life. Kevin comes up behind me and wraps his arms around my waist, placing his chin on my shoulder.

"Come on, babe. How about I draw you a nice bath and you can relax for a bit, huh?"

"That sounds great. Why are you so amazing?" I turn in his arms and wrap mine around the back of his neck, pulling him in for a sweet kiss on the lips. He hums his approval and deepens the kiss before pulling back and looking into my honey brown eyes.

"It's going to be fine. We'll figure everything out. When are you heading back out there?"

"Uncle Rob is going to introduce me to people this weekend, and then I'm going to have to get out there to start. Aunt Sheryl had an apartment above the bakery, so I won't have to worry about where to live. You can man the fort here for a while, and then I'll be back before you know it." I smile and continue. "There's no way I'll be able to keep that place going. Honestly, I think it's going to be best to see if I can convince Uncle Rob to take it back."

"She had an apartment there? Why?" he asks.

"I have no idea. Uncle Rob didn't even know it existed."

"Interesting. Want me to come with you this weekend?"

"Yeah, that would be great. I'm going to head back down on Friday just so I can look over everything and get a lay of the land. Plus, I want to check out the apartment to see what it has to offer."

Kevin pulls out from my embrace and walks toward the bathroom to start the water.

"Hey, Kev?" I ask, looking at the floor.

"Yeah, babe?" he asks, coming back into the room.

"It's going to be okay, right?"

He smiles and replies, "We'll figure it out, don't worry."

CHAPTER THREE

*T*he rest of the week goes by in a blur. Karen called me back to let me know the office is willing to allow remote work for a while, to see how it goes. I'm thankful, knowing that I won't have to completely uproot my life to take this unplanned adventure. The compromise is I will work days at the bakery, but I am to be available by email at all times, then I can work for a few hours in the evening at my real job. It's going to be a lot for the next several months, but I promise Karen I will be able to make it work. I have to if I eventually want my life back!

Friday comes quickly and, wanting to avoid traffic, I'm on the road to the shop early in the morning. I arrive at nine in the morning and look around. The shops around it are hustling and bustling, and the foot traffic is especially heavy for a Friday morning. Aunt Sheryl really did pick a prime location for this shop; no wonder it does so well.

I find the outside door that leads upstairs to the apartment and decide I want to check it out first. I take the keys out of my purse and locate the correct one to let me into the stairwell. Unlocking the door, my senses are filled with the heavenly aroma of chocolate and cinnamon. I smile as I think about the times Aunt Sheryl made me hot chocolate after a bad date or failed test. She insisted on adding extra whipped cream and a dash of cinnamon on those hard days.

I continue my way up the stairs and unlock the door to the actual apartment. It smells just like her home, and I find myself tearing up the more I think of her. I quickly wipe my eyes, knowing I have stuff to get done today, and begin looking around.

The front door opens into the living room. I see a small cream-colored loveseat, small coffee table, and a lamp in the corner. The carpets are a mixed grey and brown color. The wall next to the door has a small TV on a stand and a few knickknacks on the shelf. Behind the TV, there is a beautiful painting of the ocean with a sailboat on it.

I walk into the small galley kitchen and look through the cabinets, needing to familiarize myself with where everything is located. I open the fridge to look at what is in there, which isn't much. Picking up the expired milk carton, I scrunch my face in disgust before putting it back in the fridge to take care of later when I purchase new food.

I walk down the hallway to the only bedroom. The room is small with a full-sized bed, a nightstand, and a small dresser with four drawers pushed against the back wall. I open the blinds to allow sunlight into the room; the window overlooks the street. There is minimal artwork on the walls and a picture on the dresser catches my eye; I walk over and see it is a candid picture of me in the bakery. I am looking down at a bowl, a wooden spoon in my hand and flour on my cheek. I can't remember her taking pictures of me at the bakery. I run my fingers over the frame and jump when I hear a car horn blaring.

Placing the photo back down, I look out the window. There is a handsome man with chestnut hair peering into the bakery windows. I open the apartment window and screen so I can lean out and call down to him.

"Hey, the shop is closed. Can I help you with something?"

"Oh, um, I was looking for Sheryl. Is she just on vacation?" He looks up, shielding his ocean blue eyes from the sun above.

"Hang on, I'll be right down." I close the screen and window and lock it tight before heading down the stairs to the street. I push open the door, and the man walks over to me. He is tall, about six-feet, and has a chiseled jaw and a small dimple in his chin. "Sheryl passed away unexpectedly," I respond.

He looks down at his feet and shoves his hands in his front pockets before meeting my gaze again. "Oh, I'm sorry to hear that. Were you close to her?"

"Yeah, I'm her niece. She was like a second mom; she was there for everything. Who are you?" I ask, admiring his handsome features.

"Just an old friend. I wanted to say hi. Don't worry about it. Sorry to bother you." He turns and starts walking down the street away from me.

"Bye," I say quietly as I open the street door to go back into the apartment. I admire his backside as he continues down the street away from me. *I'm allowed to look, just can't touch.*

I finish my walk-through of the apartment and lock up before heading down into the shop. It has been a long time since I have visited the shop—too long. Aunt Sheryl was constantly asking me to come and help; I always told her I didn't have time and I was too busy. Looking around the shop now makes me regret that decision, and a pang of guilt runs through me. It's real. She's gone and I have nothing left.

I pull a chair down from one of the small tables and crumple into it, finally letting the tears fall freely from my eyes as I place my head in my arms. This isn't fair; I'm not supposed to lose her, too. *She was supposed to be here for everything!* I'm supposed to be in the city with Kevin, happy, loving my life and job. This is going to be so hard on Kevin and I. He has been wonderful and understanding, but I notice things have been different since breaking the news to him.

I sit up a short while later after I'm done feeling sorry for myself. *No use crying over spilled milk.* I take a deep, steadying breath and walk out, locking the shop up behind me. I need to get some groceries and get over to Uncle Rob's house so I can make him a proper dinner. I know he hasn't had a proper meal since Aunt Sheryl passed away. Even though he has about one hundred casseroles in the freezer from many of his neighbors and friends, I want to make him something fresh.

The grocery store is practically empty when I arrive, and I find a parking spot directly in front. *Must be my lucky day!* I pull the list from my purse and take a cart to move around the store with. I move up and down the aisles slowly, crossing items off my list as I go. I am looking for a can of crushed tomatoes and see it's perched on the top shelf, pushed back, out of reach of my short frame. I sigh heavily and begin looking for someone taller to help get it for me when I notice the man from outside the bakery.

"Hey, excuse me," I ask, tapping him on the shoulder. "Are you able to get that can for me?" I motion toward the requested item on the top shelf.

He smiles and nods his head. "Sure." He reaches up, his shirt lifting just enough to reveal some of his defined stomach muscles as he brings the item back down and places it in my hands.

"Thank you so much. It sucks being short in the grocery store." I laugh quietly as I place the item in my cart. "I never caught your name earlier. I'm Kaylan Santine." I stick my hand out for a shake.

"Jack Madison," he responds, returning the gesture. "It's nice to meet you."

"Likewise. You never did tell me how you knew my aunt?" I

ask, trying to strike up a casual conversation, but also to answer the burning question.

"An old friend, like I said before. She helped me out a few times." His gaze falls to his feet. "She was a great lady, and I'm sorry for your loss. Is the bakery opening again?"

"Yeah, it's opening again tomorrow morning. I'm going to be taking charge for a few months until I can convince my uncle that we need to sell the place."

His eyes lock with mine as soon as I say *sell the place*, an unspoken question hanging in the air.

"I can't manage the shop. I live in the city, have a job, an apartment. I can't drop everything just because my aunt said *jump*." The words spill out before I can stop them. *Why am I telling this strange man my personal business?*

"Hmm," he manages to mutter, the air between us now thick.

"Listen, I've gotta get going. I'm making dinner for my uncle tonight. Thanks for the help. I'll see you around, okay?" I tell him, pushing my cart away from him to finish my shopping. The conversation was weird, and I dwell on it the rest of the time in the store and on my way to the apartment. *Why does he care if I sell the bakery?* I am very curious as to who he is and how he knew Aunt Sheryl. I'm going to have to ask Uncle Rob to see if he knows Jack.

I carry the groceries up the stairs, managing it all in one trip, and put them away, removing the expired food as I do so. The apartment is cozy, and I smile as I pour a glass of wine and move to the bedroom to put my clothes away. I open the dresser drawer and find a few men's clothes in there. I scrunch my face in confusion as I pull them out to examine them; two pairs of dark wash jeans, a couple of black V-neck t-shirts, a navy blue sweater, and a pair of basketball shorts.

The sizing looks wrong to belong to Uncle Rob; he isn't the largest of men, but there is no way he's a size thirty-two waist.

Maybe they are his from many years ago. I shrug and place the clothes in the closet so I have use of all the drawers. Once I unpack my clothes, I move into the bathroom to unpack my make-up, hair care products, and tools.

I look at the clock on the wall, grab the grocery items needed to make dinner from the counter, and place the empty glass of wine down. I lock up and make the short ride over to Rob's house. As I park the car, he walks out the front door and smiles brightly.

"Hey, hun, can I help you carry stuff in?" he asks as I begin pulling the items out of the trunk.

"Yeah, that'd be great. Can you take these?" I hand him a few bags. He grabs them and makes his way to the front door, holding it open for me to walk through. I thank him and go into the kitchen to start preparing dinner.

"I'm gonna make chicken parmesan. Are you okay with that?" I ask.

"That sounds great, thanks. You know you don't have to go through all this trouble, right? I have enough leftovers in my freezer that I can eat. I'm not completely incompetent, you know." He laughs as he takes a seat at the table.

"I know, I just figure you're sick of eating tuna noodle casserole. I imagine you've been eating it for the past week now."

"Yeah, that and macaroni and cheese. People sure love their noodle dishes, that's for sure." He trails off.

"Hey, you alright?" I ask, looking over my shoulder at him.

"I just miss her so damn much. I can't believe she's gone. The only things I have left of her are in this house and the bakery. I don't know what I'll do if you sell it. I know she wanted to keep it in the family... it meant so much to her," he responds, looking into my eyes as he tucks a strand of sandy blonde hair behind my ear and cups my cheek.

"I know, Uncle Rob. I told you I'd give it a few months, see what happens. If it means that much to you, I can pass the reins over to you and then it can stay in the family." I place a reassuring hand on his shoulder as I gave a small smile.

"Sweetheart," he starts placing his hand over mine, "I'm getting old. She wanted you to have it because she hoped you'd pass it down to your kids, and they could pass it on. This was never about me; it's always been about you. I know this is a lot for you to handle and process, but I would really like to make this work." He stands and walks to the fridge, pulling a beer out and offering it to me, but I shake my head no. "Let's not worry about it right now. We'll see how the next couple of months go and take it from there."

I nod my head in agreement and start cooking dinner for the two of us. Chicken parmesan is one of my favorites, and I can make this dish blindfolded. I'm on autopilot as my mind works overtime playing the *what if* game. What if I fail? What if the shop goes under? What if I love it? What if...

What if I want to stay?

Would Kevin be willing to move out here? I sigh heavily as I finish cooking the chicken and plate the dishes.

"Uncle Rob, dinner's ready," I call for him. He is outside on the porch talking with some neighbors. He walks through the door and smiles at me.

"It smells wonderful in here. Thank you, sweetheart, for doing this" He takes a seat and picks up his fork and knife.

"I brought some cookies for dessert, too."

His eyes light up at the prospect of sweets. "Did you make them?" he asks, excitement in his voice.

"No, um," I hesitate. "I bought them from the bakery at the store." I watch as the light in his eyes diminishes and his facial features fall.

"Oh, right. You wouldn't have had time to make any. Not sure what I was thinking. Sorry."

The rest of dinner is mostly silent. I can hear the birds

chirping outside and the trees rustling as the wind blows gently. It's relaxing here, much different than the city. I feel like I could actually relax, read a book, take a nap. I can do all the things I never do because I'm always on the move. I sigh as I think about what to do.

CHAPTER FOUR

y plan is to head down to the bakery around nine to meet with the employees, but around four in the morning, noise from below wakes me up. I decide I might as well get an early start. I throw on a t-shirt and a pair of yoga pants, pulling my wavy locks into a messy bun. After making a large tumbler of coffee, I head down into the bakery. The music is blaring, and the kitchen is warm, a sign the ovens have been on for a while.

I walk behind the counter and see a robust woman in her mid-fifties adding ingredients into an industrial-sized mixer, her back toward me. I find the volume for the radio and turn it down, causing her to jump and place her hand over her heart. She turns off the mixer and wipes her hands on her apron, extending one to shake mine. I take it and smile at her.

She smiles. "Morning, dear, I'm Denise. I wasn't expecting you here until later. Why are you here so early?"

"Hi, I'm Kaylan. The music woke me up," I say, stifling a yawn. She has the good grace to flush a little.

"Sorry, normally, no one is in that apartment and the music

helps me get going in the mornings. I'll try to keep it down from now on."

"It's fine. What are you making anyway?" I ask, walking closer to the mixer to see what's inside.

"I'm making whoopie pies right now, and then I have to make cream puffs, white chocolate chunk, raspberry, macadamia cookies, and éclairs." She turns the mixer on while I continue to stand there staring at her in amazement. *That is a lot of stuff to make in one morning!*

"Holy shit, that's a lot. Do you do this every morning?" I practically yell over the mixer's motor to be heard.

"Normally, I have less to do, but since the shop's been closed the last two weeks, I have a lot to catch up on." She motions toward the large fridge. "You can start forming the cake balls if you want to help. I've already added the frosting to the crumbled cake; you just need to form them so we can dip them."

She returns to her work, and I walk over to the fridge and take a large chafing dish out, which is filled with chocolate cake. She must have been here for a lot longer than I realize because there is no way she did all this work in one hour. I turn to look at her, and she is dancing her way around the kitchen. I chuckle and shake my head. *At least she seems happy.*

"What do you want me to put these on?" I ask, looking around for something to use.

"See that large container over there?" She points to a shelf that houses a deep clear plastic container. "Grab that and put some parchment paper in it. You're going to stack them, so you need parchment in between each layer."

I nod my head in understanding and walk to the sink to wash up before I start. Forming balls isn't going to be too hard. I can do this. I dry my hands on a towel and walk back to the table, digging my fingers into the sticky mess. The feel of the cake is strange but not unpleasant as I squish it through my fingers, giving it a test squeeze. I pull a small amount from the dish and start rolling the dough between my palms, placing the ball in the container when I'm done. I pick up another small amount of dough and do it again. I continue this process until the bottom layer is filled. When I look at what I've made though, all of them seem to be different sizes. I huff annoyance and look over at Denise.

"Hey, Denise, how do I make these all the same size? These look horrible. No one's going to want these." I wipe my hands on my apron and take a sip of coffee. She walks over and looks at the cake balls over my shoulder and laughs.

"Oh, dear, no those aren't very good, are they?" I feel my face heat up from embarrassment. She turns toward a drawer, pulls out a cookie scoop, and hands it to me. "Why don't you try using this to measure out the dough and then form the ball? That will probably be better."

"Did Aunt Sheryl used to make these by hand?" I ask as I start all over again, using the scoop this time.

"Oh, yeah, she was quick at them, too. She'd been making them for years and knew just from holding it in her hands if they were the right size or not. She was the queen of making cake balls, so none of us ever did it. We would just help dip in the chocolate afterward." She finishes mixing everything and begins placing large spoonsful of batter onto parchment lined cookie sheets, lining them up next to the oven. Once all four cookie sheets are full, she places them in the oven and turns on the timer, quickly filling more trays.

I seem to be moving at a glacial pace in comparison, and it makes me feel useless. By the time I finish using all the dough to roll the balls, Denise is on to another task, having cleaned up the mess. She's moved all the whoopie pies to a cooling rack. I look at the clock on the wall and it reads five fifty-four. All I have accomplished in almost an hour is making cake balls, and I haven't even completed that; they still needed to be dipped in chocolate. I groan inwardly. I'm never going to get the hang of this. Denise notices the inner war I'm having with myself because she comes over and places a reassuring hand on my shoulder.

"Dear, we all have to start somewhere. You'll get it. Remember, I've been doing this for ten years, and your aunt had been doing it a lot longer. We've had more practice than you, so don't be so hard on yourself."

"I get that. It's just I can normally pick things up quickly and figured this would be the same." I take another sip of my coffee, allowing the warm liquid to soothe my worries. "Are you here every morning doing this?" I turn my head so I can look at her face on.

"Yes, I am. Your aunt and I made a good team. I have a feeling you and I will make a good team, too. Just be patient. I'll teach you everything I know, okay?"

I smile and nod my head in agreement. "Yeah, that sounds great. Listen, I'm going to be back in a little while. Are you okay if I leave for a bit?" I watch as her features fall slightly in disappointment before I continue. "I'm still working my other job, too, and I have to be able to get some of that done, along with this." I make a sweeping motion around the kitchen with my arm.

"I understand, let me show you show you how to finish the cake balls, then you can take a break, okay?"

I smile and nod my head in agreement. Dipping the cake balls is a lot easier than forming them. I place one on the dipper, watch it disappear beneath the gooey, melted chocolate, and pull it back up. I place it down on a parchment lined cookie sheet and watch as the chocolate begins to harden, giving it a nice gloss. One after another, I dip them until I'm finished. I smile, happy with what I have accomplished, and turn toward Denise.

"Cake balls are done. I'm going to head upstairs to get some of my other job done now."

"Sure, honey. I'll see you in a bit. Jessica gets here at eight-thirty so we can open at nine. When are you coming back?"

"Uncle Rob wanted to bring me in at nine, so I guess I'll be back then. That gives me a few hours to get cleaned up and get some work done. I'll see you then." I wave as I walk out of the kitchen and back upstairs to the apartment.

I pick up my phone and text Kevin. He is probably at the gym so I know he won't be able to talk.

Me: *Good morning, handsome. I miss you. I just wanted to say have a great day. What time are you getting here?*

A few minutes pass as I sip my coffee, feet pulled under me on the couch.

Kevin: *Morning. I should be there around 11 today. See you then.*

I smile at the message and pick up my laptop to start some work. I figure I can get about two hours in before I have to get ready. I open my emails and click through, answering any that are urgent. The time flies by, and when I look at the wall clock, it is already eight-thirty. *Shit!* I wanted to stop at eight so I'd have time to shower, put on makeup, and style my hair. I guess I will have to settle for a quick shower and a messy bun.

I jump up, turn on the water for the shower, and strip down. I stick my hand under the water waiting for it to get warm. Something isn't right though; the water has been running for at least two minutes, and it's still freezing. I wrap a towel around myself and walk into the kitchen to turn on that water, too. The same thing happens; the only water coming out is cold.

"Gah!" I scream in frustration, turning off the water. Guess a shower isn't happening. I make a mental note to contact the landlord to have it fixed. I pull on a pair of skinny jeans and a Red Sox baseball t-shirt and walk back into the bathroom to do my hair and makeup. *Thank goodness for dry shampoo!* Maybe I can use Uncle Rob's shower until this one gets fixed. I pull my hair into a ponytail and wrap it into a messy bun with the last loop of the elastic, effectively keeping it out of my face.

I exit the apartment and head back down into the street, where Uncle Rob is getting ready to buzz to go upstairs.

"Hey, sweetheart, sleep okay?" he asks as he pulls me into a hug.

"Yeah, I slept fine. Denise woke me up this morning though. The music was a bit loud."

He laughs and cups his hand on my shoulder. "Yeah, Sheryl used to yell at her for that, too. You'll get used to it." The two of us walk into the bakery and I looked around. The display cases are filled with all sorts of treats—cookies, cake balls, whoopie pies, cream puffs, and éclairs. *How is it even possible to make all of this so quickly?* My eyes are bugging out of my head, and Denise looks at me and laughs.

"Girl, you better get used to seeing all of this. You'll see them every morning now," she says as she walks out from behind the counter to greet the two of us. "Hey, Rob, how ya doing?" she asks, pulling him into a hug.

"I'm okay, thanks for asking," he responds, hugging her back before standing up straight again. "Heard your music was loud this morning and woke this one up." He jerks his thumb in my direction.

"Yeah, well, when it's a good song, I just have to shake my booty. You know I like my music loud, Rob." She laughs.

"Come on, let me introduce you to Jessica," she says, lightly slapping my arm and motioning for me to follow her. We walk around the counter, and I see a girl in her early twenties smiling as she checks a customer out. "Jessica dear, this is Kaylan. Kaylan, this is Jessica."

I reach my hand out to shake hers. "It's nice to meet you."

"Kaylan is taking over the shop, so we need to show her the ropes," Denise declares. I nod my head yes and smile at Jessica. I could have sworn her smile faltered for a moment, but when I look again, her smile is as bright as before. I leave Jessica behind the counter to attend to the customers in the shop. Denise, Rob, and I walk into the back office to talk.

"I have so many questions and concerns about doing this. I don't even know where to start. Until this morning, I hadn't baked in a kitchen since I was in college and I'm not entirely comfortable doing so. Denise, I think you fit this role much better than I could," I ramble, my arms taking on a life of their own.

"Kaylan," she tries interrupting, as I continue my speech. "Kaylan," she repeats louder in a sing-song voice, gaining my attention. I blush and close my mouth to let her speak. "All you need to know is if it tastes good, it will sell. Your aunt spent her life getting this small shop on the map in this town. Come in with me every day, and I'll teach you the recipes. She has them all written down, but she never used them, said she liked to bake from the heart. I called bullshit and told her she had them memorized so she could burn the evidence when the cops came sniffing around."

I choke while swallowing and start coughing. "Excuse me?" I ask, hitting my chest with my palm, trying to ease my coughing fit.

"Oh, hun, I'm just kidding. People have said that her baking was so good that cocaine must be baked into it." She laughs boisterously. "You're family. You can do this. I know you can." She smiles reassuringly.

I huff, conceding. "I may have to stop on and off. As I told you this morning, I'm still working my other job, too, and my boyfriend is coming into town on the weekends. Oh," I say loudly, making everyone jump. "I need the number for the landlord. There's no hot water upstairs in the apartment. Do you have the number?"

"It's somewhere in here, dear. The landlord is a guy named John Petersen. Why don't you take a few minutes to look around while I talk to Rob?"

"Sure, thanks. Oh, also, Uncle Rob, do you have contact info for Dan? I'd like to set something up with him."

"I'm sure I do. If not, it's probably there in the office. Check the Rolodex. His last name is Levy." He points to a Rolodex on a shelf. I must have given a funny look because he laughs quietly and says, "You know your aunt wasn't into technology."

"Yeah, that's for sure," I mutter as I pull it down and start rummaging through the cards with numbers, Rob and Denise leaving me alone. Flipping back to the "P" section, I locate John Petersen's card and pick up the phone to dial his number. The phone rings three times before switching over to voicemail. I am slightly annoyed but leave a message anyway.

"Hi, John, my name is Kaylan. I'm Sheryl Albert's niece. I am staying in the apartment upstairs from the bakery, and when I tried to shower today, there was no hot water. If you could please call me back, I'd appreciate it. Thank you." I leave my phone number and hang up, hoping he will call back sooner than later.

I look down at my phone as I watch a few emails come in from work. I swear these people never sleep. I take a few minutes to respond and sigh heavily; this is going to be a long couple of months. I tuck my phone back into my pocket and leave the office, trying to keep a migraine at bay. I notice Denise and Rob in a heated discussion.

"What do you want me to do about it, Denise? I'll talk to Dan, find out what's going on," he says hastily.

"Everything okay? What are you guys talking about?" I ask, making my presence known.

Rob takes a step back from Denise and drops his hands. Denise smiles and nods her head at me before looking back at Rob. "We'll discuss this more later." She turns to face me again. "It's nothing of importance, Kaylan. Now, do you want to help me do more baking, or are there other matters you have to attend to?"

If it is nothing important, then why are they arguing about it? I tilt my head to the side and smile. "I can help you now. Kevin should be here in about an hour so I have some time."

"Great, grab an apron. We're running low on cookies. I think we should make oatmeal raisin next; it was one of your aunt's biggest sellers." She continues rambling on as I pull the apron over my head. Rob smiles tightly and motions toward the door, letting me know he is leaving. I wave bye and start paying attention to Denise again. "All the recipes are kept up here." She stretches and pulls a small box from a high shelf. You'll know them by heart in no time, and you won't have to look at them again. Why don't you look through them while I get the ingredients together, hmm?" she suggests as she begins bringing ingredients over to the table.

I start looking through all the recipes and can't wrap my head around how someone could memorize all of these. The one thing I remember about baking is it's like chemistry; everything has to be measured or else it won't come out correctly. The fact that she was able to remember how many cups of flour went into cream puffs verses whoopie pies is impressive.

"Denise, do you have to use the recipes, or do you have them memorized as well?"

Without even stopping what she's doing, she responds, "I've been making them almost as long as your aunt. I have them mostly memorized. I do have to look on occasion, as I can't always remember if I am supposed to add baking soda or baking powder."

"There is no way I'll ever be able to remember all of these," I mumble as I look through all the sweet treats. The basics are there—the cookies, éclairs, and whoopie pies—but there are also some that don't seem familiar to me. I worked in the shop on and off for a few years, but I don't ever recall seeing Venetian cookies or coffee cake being sold. "I don't think I've ever seen some of these recipes made here. Tried and failed?" I ask, sorting through more of them.

"Yeah, some of them just didn't sell well, while some of them take too long to make so they were made as a special treat on occasion. Can you come help me crack these eggs into the butter and sugar mix?"

"Sure." I close the box and put it on the shelf again before walking over to the mixer.

"You know, she talked about you all the time. You were the daughter she never had. I understand why she left the shop to you. This isn't going to be the easiest thing, but it is rewarding." She is trying hard to sell me on the place. She keeps talking, and I find myself tuning her out as I listen to the motor of the mixer and the hum of the oven. The kitchen is getting warmer by the minute, and I feel sweat forming on my brow. I pull my phone from my pocket and see I had five new emails. I push my breath through my nose and pocket the phone again.

"Hey, Denise, I'm gonna take a few minutes if that's okay. It's getting hot in here, and I need to check on work as well."

"Yeah, I have a lot to teach you, so if you are able to come back and help, it would be appreciated." She continues working, not even batting an eye at me. I take the apron off and walk out into the front of the store. I notice Jessica smile at a customer as she is handing his change back to him. I look up at his chiseled face and recognize Jack immediately. I give him a small smile as he takes a seat to dig into this éclair.

"Hey, Jack, right?" I ask, placing my hands on the back of the empty chair at his small table. He looks up at me and smiles brightly, motioning for me to take a seat.

"These are my favorite." He picks up the pastry and takes a large bite from it. A low moan escapes his mouth as he chews the sweet dessert, and I feel a tingle in the pit of my stomach.

"That good, huh?" I ask, raising my eyebrows in surprise.

"Yeah, that good. Haven't you had them before?" I shake my head no and he guffaws. "You own the place and you've never had the best thing behind the counter?"

I blush and play with the hem of my shirt. "I, um," I pause for a moment. "I try to avoid sugary sweets. I used to be a lot heavier than I am, so I'm careful about what I eat." *Why did I feel like I had to tell him that?*

Clearly, he can tell he hit a nerve, and he immediately begins trying to backpedal. "Well, you, um... you look great. You should think about adding it back into rotation every now and again. Want a bite of mine?" he asks as he slides the plate in front of me.

I feel my cheeks begin to flush, and the bell above the door signals someone entering.

"Here you are, Kaylan. I've been texting you," Kevin says, walking over to me and placing a kiss on the top of my head. I look up at him and smile. "Should you be having that?" he asks, looking at the éclair on the small plate.

"Oh, no, it's Jack's," I reply, sliding the plate back in front of him. "Jack, this is my boyfriend, Kevin. Kevin, this is Jack. He's a friend of my aunt's," I introduce them. Jack sticks his hand out for Kevin to shake and he takes it begrudgingly.

"Nice to meet you," they say in unison.

My phone rings, and an unknown number flashes on the caller

ID. "Shit, sorry, hang on," I apologize as I answer the phone. "Hello? Yes, this is her. Oh, great, you can come by in an hour? That would be perfect. Yes, I'll meet you upstairs. Thanks." I hang up the phone and turn to see the boys awkwardly looking around the shop, avoiding each other. "The landlord is coming in an hour to fix the hot water." I smile, thinking about how nice a warm shower will feel.

"What's wrong with the water?" Kevin asks, confused.

"It doesn't work. It was just cold when I tried it."

"Put the cold water on. I bet it will get warm," Jack interjects and takes another bite of his éclair, eyes locked on Kevin.

"That doesn't make sense. We'll wait for the landlord to look at it," Kevin says.

"Jack, you may be on to something. The water lines may have gotten crossed somehow; it is an old building. I'll try it and see for now anyway. Thanks." I smile at him.

"Great, now that's settled, can you let me into the apartment? I want to drop my stuff off, and I have some work I need to get done," Kevin says.

"Oh, yeah, sure." I turn to look at Jack. "Thanks for the advice. Enjoy the éclair." Kevin and I walk out of the bakery and head toward the stairs for the apartment. I look in through the window and see Jack watching me walk by, a smile playing at the corner of his lips. I smile to myself and walk up the stairs to the apartment.

CHAPTER FIVE

"I'm happy you could come. I miss you," I say, pulling Kevin into a hug when he drops his bags inside the apartment.

"I've missed you, too, Kaylan, but it's only been two days," he replies, closing his arms around me and kissing the top of my head. "Where's the bedroom? I want to put my stuff away so I can get some work done."

I drop my arms from around his waist and point down the hall. I let out a small sigh before I speak up. "I was hoping I could show you some of the town. This town was my second home growing up so I know it fairly well."

"Maybe in a little bit, is that okay? I've got a huge deadline I'm trying to meet. I figure maybe we can do dinner or something later?" he asks, poking his head out from the room, smiling at me.

"Yeah, that would fine. I should try to get some work done, too. I have a couple of emails I have to get through anyway, and then Denise needs me to get back down into the bakery." I pull my laptop into my lap, opening it to start on more work. I checked my emails not too long ago, and my inbox is already getting flooded with more requests. *Don't these people ever take a break?* I think as I hit reply to my fifth message.

The day goes by quickly. The landlord stops by, and just like Jack said, the lines are switched around. He would have to get a plumber in to fix it, and I agree to put the temperature on cold to avoid the cost. I figure I won't be around for more than a few months and can deal with that. I'm happy to know I will be able to take a shower soon though. I work throughout the day, running back and forth between the bakery and the apartment, trying to juggle both jobs. Before I know it, I look outside and the sun is lower in the sky, beginning to set for the night. Looking at the clock on the wall, the time reads six thirty-five. The shop is closed at this hour, and I stretch, feeling my back crack as I do so.

"Hey, babe, want to go get some food? I'm starving," I comment as I walk toward the bedroom, seeing him propped up on the bed, laptop in his lap.

"Yeah, food sounds great. Are there any restaurants in this town?"

"Yeah, there are a few diners here, and then it's basic fast food places. Are you in the mood for something special?"

"Diners?" he asks as he scrunches his face in disgust. "Nothing better than that?"

"What's your problem exactly? You've been a pissy all day," I accuse, crossing my arms over my chest.

He sucks in a deep breath and lets it out slowly as he tries to get his thoughts in order. Finally, after a moment of staring blankly at me, he says, "Sorry, I'm just not into small towns. You know I didn't have the best experience growing up, and small towns just seem to bring it all back."

As he's talking, I drop my hands to my side, my facial features softening at his words. He rarely talks about growing up, but I know it was difficult for him. The constant bullying and the fact his dad walked out on him and his family didn't help. I walk up to the side of the bed and sit down on the edge, resting my hand on his arm.

"Hey, I know you prefer the city, but things aren't so bad here. No one knows you here and you aren't staying for long periods of time. Can't we pretend this is a small vacation and try to enjoy it?" I offer a warm smile. "I know you aren't going to be able to come out every weekend, but maybe some weekends I can get off to come home to you. We will trade off or something. We can talk every day. Like you said last week, we'll figure it all out." He smiles at me and nods his head in agreement. "Now, a few towns over, there's a great restaurant that just opened—*Red Bird*. It's supposed to have excellent food. How about we get on something nice and we can head over?"

"Yeah, that sounds great," he beams and leans forward to kiss me on the lips.

THE RESTAURANT IS everything and more. The mood is relaxing yet sophisticated, and the food is exquisite. I get the brown butter, three-cheese ravioli with hints of sage, and he gets the chicken piccata with fresh green beans and mashed potatoes.

"We are coming here every time I come out to visit," he announces as he places his fork down, leaning back in his chair for a small stretch. "I want to talk to the owner, see if he's thought of expanding into other places. I think this would be a great place to have close to us, don't you agree?"

I am only half paying attention to him, my body yelling at me to go to sleep. It is only about eight, but I am so tired, I think I might pass out at the table.

"Earth to Kaylan," Kevin says, waving his hand in front of my face.

I blink a few times until my eyes focus on him again, and I

smile shyly. "Sorry, I'm just so tired. Yeah, the food was excellent here." He waves toward the hostess to gain her attention and asks to leave his number for the owner to call him back. She is hesitant but takes his card and tells him she will pass it along to the manager to give to the owners. Kevin smiles at her as she walks away.

He pays the check, and we make our way back to the apartment. With my head resting on the headrest of the car, my eyes flutter closed on the short ride back.

He gently shakes me awake. "Kaylan, wake up. We're back."

I groan a little and begrudgingly open my eyes, looking around and smiling at him. "Sorry, I have to be up again early tomorrow, so I'm just going to go straight to bed. Feel free to stay up and watch TV or something."

I lean over and give him a kiss on the cheek before I open the door and get out and head up the stairs to the apartment. He follows suit and closes the front door quietly behind him as I make my way to the bedroom. Changing quickly, I set the alarm, and as soon as my head hits the pillow, I'm out like a light.

At two in the morning, I wake in a panic and look around frantically before I recognize where I am and calm down. The dream that startled me awake is fading from my memory, and I lay in bed for a few minutes before I decide to get up. I take a quick shower, the hot water cascading over my body, helping wake me up. I want to stay under the hot stream for a long time, but know I will have to go down to the shop soon and think better of it. I quickly wash up and step out, getting dressed in a green t-shirt, yoga capris, and a pair of sneakers. I pile my hair on top of my head and head back into the room to shut off the alarm.

Kevin is still in a deep sleep, and I don't want to wake him up, so I quietly leave the apartment and head down to the shop to get an early start, hoping I won't mess anything up on my own. I lock the front door behind me and walk into the kitchen, turning on the lights and the oven. I figure I can start with something easy like cookies. *How badly can I mess these up?* I reach up for the recipe box and pull the recipe out for chocolate chunk cookies. These were always my favorite, and I smile at the memories of Aunt Sheryl handing me one, freshly baked.

I turn the radio on to a classic rock station, remembering to turn it down to not wake Kevin. Dancing around the kitchen, I gather the ingredients listed on the recipe card. The butter is added to the mixer along with the sugar, and I start it up, watching as it turns into a yellow, creamy, mix. I add the eggs and vanilla and then slowly add the flour mixture, watching as the beater tries to work through the thickening batter before turning it up a notch. Finally, when I can't see any streaks of flour, I add the chocolate chunks and give it a quick mix.

Turning off the mixer, I take a small amount of the batter between my thumb and forefinger before popping the sugary mix into my mouth and closing my eyes, savoring the flavor.

"You gonna just stand there with a goofy look on your face, or are you actually gonna bake the darn things?" Denise asks, making me jump, not realizing she came into the room.

"I'm gonna bake the darn things, as you so put it. I just want to make sure they taste good first. These were always my favorite," I tell her as I pull out the baking sheets and the large cookie scooper.

She walks over to the recipe card and picks it up before looking at me. "You know, your aunt stopped making these when you moved to the city. She said because they were your favorite, she only wanted to make them when you came around. Any time you were coming to visit, she would make sure some were in the case."

I look over at her, and I can see her eyes glistening. I feel my chin start to quiver and the tears begin to form. "I didn't know she did that," I practically whisper.

"Yeah, she wanted it to be something special for you." She wipes her eyes and clears her throat. "Anyway, I think she would be thrilled that you decided to make this cookie."

"Denise, I stopped eating sugary stuff a long time ago. All those times I came to visit I never once took one of these cookies. She would offer them to me, but I would never take them, always giving her an excuse. I feel like such as ass." A tear rolls down my cheek, and I brush it away quickly, turning my head so Denise can't see me crying.

"Kaylan, honey, she was never mad at you for not taking one. She loved you just the way you are, and she would hate that you're feeling this way right now," she responds, pulling me into a tight embrace. "She would be so proud of you, stepping up and doing this, learning how to run her bakery. It was her baby. She was happiest when she was here." She pulls back and gives me a happy smile, giving my arms a light squeeze before dropping them. "Anyway, let's get these in the oven. We have a lot more to do."

With Denise's help, I get all the cookies on the sheets and the pans in the ovens before starting the next thing. "What do you want to learn next?"

"I would love to learn how to make éclairs. Can you teach me those?" The words leave my mouth before I actually have a chance to register them. I keep picturing Jack eating his yesterday, and how happy he looked, and how delicious the eclair looked. *I'm with Kevin. Why am I thinking about Jack?* I push the thought from my mind and tell myself it's because the treat is popular with customers and I need to learn them eventually.

Denise pulls the card out of the box, and I start gathering everything we need, the two of us working in tandem. A clean mixing bowl is put under the mixer, and it's turned back on. She starts walking me through the process. It seems relatively easy until I have to actually put them on the baking sheet.

"Okay, so you are just going to pipe it into a straight line about four inches long like this." Denise demonstrates, her left hand guiding the bag and the right hand squeezing the mixture out onto the sheet. "Easy, right?" she asks, handing the bag over to me to give it a try.

I follow her instructions and try, failing miserably. The first part comes out of the bag too thick and spreads out while the end is so thin, and the whole thing is only about three inches long. "This looks horrible." I laugh as I lift the bag up from the cookie sheet. Denise scrunches her face and laughs at my failed attempt.

"Looks like you added too much pressure at the beginning and not enough at the end. That's okay. That one can be for you or Kevin. It won't look pretty but I bet it will taste great! Try again, and make sure you pipe it out with even pressure the whole time."

I take a deep breath and push it out through my nose quickly. "Kevin won't eat this. He tries to avoid sweets, too. Maybe we can give it to some poor, unsuspecting person." I chuckle.

"How about you give that bad one to the handsome man that was here the other day? He seemed interested in you."

"Jack? No, he's a friend of Aunt Sheryl's." I pick up the bag and try again, my brows creasing from concentration. I hold the bag up and look at the mostly straight line. "Hey, this doesn't look too bad!" I smile triumphantly and raise my hand to Denise for a high five.

"Hmm, I've never seen him around before," she replies and shrugs her shoulders. "Great job, now you just need to do fifteen more just like that and we will be good to go."

I try my hardest, and while they aren't perfect, they aren't too bad. I figure they will be okay to sell. We get those in the oven and get the mess cleaned up to start the cream filling. Glancing at the clock, I notice it is already five-thirty, and I figure Kevin will be getting up to go for a run.

"Denise, is it okay if I take a break? I want to catch Kevin before he leaves for his run this morning."

"Sure. I need to show you how to make the filling and the ganache for the éclairs as well, so come back." She looks back at the bowl and starts cooking the eggs and sugar over the double boiler. I take off my apron and run upstairs. When I enter the apartment, I notice him sitting on the couch tying his sneakers.

"Oh, good, I caught you. Morning, babe," I say, leaning over and giving him a quick peck on the lips.

"Mmm, you taste like sugar and chocolate. Hope you aren't eating too many sweets down there," he replies, standing and picking up his headphones. The little comments are getting old quick, and I'm getting annoyed.

"What if I ate the whole batch of cookies? What would you say about that?" I cross my arms, my posture in a defensive stance.

"That's not what I meant and you know it, Kaylan." I watch as he rolls his eyes at me and gives me a quick kiss on the cheek. "I'm going to have to leave early today. I have a lot of stuff I need to finish so I would rather us not be fighting. I just know you've worked really hard to look the way you do, and I'd hate to see you upset at yourself because you are now working in a bakery." He reaches for the handle of the door and pulls it open. "I'll make sure to stop by before I leave." He closes the door, leaving me standing there alone.

The past two days, he's made comments about me eating sugary treats and I'm beyond frustrated. I'm working in a Goddamn bakery, so if I decide to have a cookie or two, it's not going to kill me. I storm back down the stairs, mumbling to myself when I push the door to the kitchen open.

"What's got your panties in a twist? You look angry," Denise comments as she watches me pick up a chocolate chunk cookie from the cooling rack and break a piece off before shoving it into my mouth.

"Kevin. I have no idea what his problem is. The past two days, he's made comments about me eating sweets like it's going to be the end all be all. If I want to have one Goddamn cookie, I'm going to!" I practically yell. I drop my head and shake it back and forth gently. "Sorry, Denise, that was rude of me. You didn't deserve that. I just need to vent."

"Any reason why he's saying stuff like that?"

"I was a bit heavier when we started dating, and he got me into working out and eating healthy. Not that my eating was terrible before, but he helped me make better choices. I lost several inches and got into great shape. I think he knows I am happier the size I am now and doesn't want to see me gain it back. I wish he'd back off a bit though. It's been one weekend." I break another piece of the cookie off and shove it into my mouth. "This is the best cookie I've ever had," I moan as I chew. "Who knew I could make something this amazing?"

"Cookies do make everything better. You'll work it out with Kevin," she pauses for a moment, "if you want to. Anyway, we've got a lot more work to do, so if you're done with that cookie, let's get back to work. Can you hand me that cut up chocolate?" She points to the cutting board with a bunch of chocolate on it. I bring it over to her, and she adds it to the mixture in the pot. The rich smell of the chocolate overpowers my senses, and I start salivating.

The rest of the morning is uneventful, and once the shop is open, I decide to head to the front to learn how to run the register and how to help the customers. The more time I spend talking with Jessica, the more I like her. She is several years younger than I, but I can tell she truly enjoys working in the shop. She is pleasant to the customers, and many of them knew her name, which tells me these customers come in frequently.

Kevin comes down around ten, showered and in a polo and shorts. "Hey, I'm heading back to the city. I just wanted to say bye before I go. Can you talk for a minute?"

"Yeah, sure." I turn to look at Jessica. "I'll be right back." I walk out from behind the counter and follow him outside.

"You know I'm only mentioning the sweets because I love you and want to see you happy, right?"

"I get that, but it's been twice in two days, Kevin. You need to give it a rest."

"No, it hasn't." He shakes his head as he scrunches his face.

"Yes, it has, Kevin. You said something yesterday about the éclair and then this morning. Just lay off a bit, will you?"

"Sorry." His reply is a bit harsh, and I flinch at the way it rolls off his tongue.

"It's fine. I have to get some more work done today anyway, and I've got to get back in there. Text me when you get home so I know you made it safe, okay?"

"Sure, we'll talk tonight." He leans over and places a small kiss on my cheek before walking toward his car. I stand on the sidewalk and wave to him as he takes off, finally turning toward the shop when he is out of sight. I feel someone entering the shop behind me and I hold the door open.

"Thanks," his honey voice responds. I turn my head and see it's Jack, a big grin on his face.

I smile back. "Coming in for another éclair?"

"Yeah, I just can't get enough of them." He pats his flat stomach and lets out a small chuckle.

"Well then, I've got one that's on the house for you, as long as you promise not to laugh at it." He makes a cross over his heart with his right index finger. "Be right back. Have a seat."

I walk back into the kitchen, take the botched éclair out of the fridge, and place it on a small plate.

"Giving that to Jack?" Denise asks, raising an eyebrow in question.

"Yeah, told him it's on the house as long as he doesn't laugh at it."

"Bet he's paying for it..." she mumbles, and I throw a towel in her direction.

"Be nice. This was my first one ever," I retort, walking back into the front of the shop. I place the pastry in front of Jack and take a seat opposite him.

"What happened to this?" He chuckles, picking up the plate to examine it from all angles before putting it back down and taking a bite out of it.

"You said you wouldn't make fun of it, remember?" I ask, an exaggerated pout on my lips.

He smiles softly and brushes his hand over mine. "I said I wouldn't laugh at it, not that I wouldn't make fun of it. If it's any consolation, it tastes just as good as it always does."

I beam up at him as he shoves the rest of it in his mouth, a small hum of appreciation coming from his lips.

CHAPTER SIX

*T*he week goes by in a blur. Between the bakery, my actual job, my uncle, and sleep, I have barely enough time to eat. I put in long days at the bakery and even longer evenings answering emails and returning calls for my other job. Karen seems happy with the amount I am able to accomplish, and I feel better that tomorrow will be Sunday again and the bakery will be closed. Last week had been an odd week because of the funeral.

Kevin isn't able to return this weekend, and I'm too tired to go home. I opt to have a quiet weekend alone, drinking wine and reading a book. I place an order for a pizza, pour myself some wine, and cuddle up on the couch under a light blanket. The open windows allow for a nice breeze through the living room. I'm just getting into a good part of the book when there is a buzz from downstairs. Figuring it is the pizza guy, I buzz him up. I fetch my wallet to pull out money, but when I open the door, Jack is standing there holding the pizza box.

"Jack, do you work at the pizza place?" I ask, taking the box from him, trying to hand him the money.

He laughs and pushes my hand away. "No, I was coming over to see if you wanted to grab a bite to eat. I know you don't have a lot of friends in the area and thought I'd be friendly and invite you. Then I saw the pizza guy standing downstairs and figured you already had dinner covered, so I thought maybe I could join you?" He looks down, and I can see the color rush to his cheeks.

"What makes you think I can't finish this pizza all by myself?" I joke.

"Oh, well…" He rubs the back of his neck, clearly embarrassed.

"I'm joking." I laugh to ease his discomfort. "I'd love the company. Come in and have a seat and I'll get some plates. Do you want anything to drink?"

"Sure. What do you have?"

"Wine, milk, water, wine, soda, wine." I laugh again.

"Wow, so many options. I guess I'll go with wine, please. Whatever you're having is fine."

I pour the wine and carry it over with the two plates and hand one to him. He opens the pizza box and takes two slices. We sit in silence, enjoying the first few bites of pizza before he asks the first question.

"Where's Kevin this weekend?"

"He couldn't make it out, and I'm too tired to make the trip out there tonight," I mumble, placing my wine glass to my lips and taking a small sip. He makes an O shape with his lips and takes another bite of his pizza.

"So, Jack, tell me a bit about yourself. What do you do for work?"

"I own a restaurant with a buddy of mine. He's the chef and I'm the brains. Well, lately, he seems to be trying to be the brains, too."

"Oh, nice, which restaurant is it?"

"*Red Bird*. Have you heard of it?"

"Oh!" I practically jump from my seat. "Yes. Kevin and I were there last week. It was wonderful; the food was to die for. I didn't know you owned it. Kevin gave his card to the hostess, trying to get it to the owner. He wanted to know if you were thinking of expanding at all. He thinks that restaurant would do well in the city."

"Hmm, well, we're trying to keep it in smaller towns, bring people out this way a bit. My buddy, Oliver, the chef, has been looking into this town possibly. He said he's been eyeing a place for a while, but the owner won't budge so he hasn't told me much else about it."

"Gotcha, that's a smart strategy. Get people to travel a bit, support small business." I take a small bite of pizza and swallow before continuing. "So, I've gotta ask, Denise has never seen you around yet you know my aunt. What's the story there?"

"I was in a sticky situation a while ago and your aunt was really nice to me. She helped me get into a good place. If it's all the same to you, it's not something I like talking about..." He trails off, uncomfortable with the topic.

"Hey, sorry, I didn't mean to cross any lines," I say, placing my hand on his knee and giving it a light pat. He places his hand over mine and gives it a gentle squeeze, the warmth of his hand causing butterflies to erupt. I pull my hand back and try to concentrate on my pizza plate, suddenly very aware as to how close he is sitting and how wonderful he smells. We sit in uncomfortable silence for another minute, avoiding eye contact. "Do you want to watch TV or something? I think there are a few movies that are here. If you want, we can play them on my laptop."

"I'm fine just talking to you unless you want to get back to reading." He motions toward the book on the end table. "I can leave if you prefer."

I smile at him. "It's nice to have friends in the area. Not to dis my uncle, but I need to be able to talk to someone my own age.

How old are you anyway? Actually, I have a lot of questions. I'd like to get to know you better."

"I'm twenty-nine, and I'd like to get to know you, too." He notices my cheeks flush, and he stumbles. "Just as friends, of course. How old are you?"

"I'm twenty-seven. Having a friend will make my lonely weeknights more exciting." I chuckle and take a bite of my pizza. "Where did you grow up?"

"I was an Army brat and I moved from state to state. My family finally settled down a few towns over, and I finished high school there before running away for college. What about you? Did you grow up here?"

I stay silent, thinking of how to respond, and lean back against the couch. "No, I grew up the next town over, but I spent most of my time with Aunt Sheryl. It was just my dad and me, and he didn't know how to raise a teenage daughter." Taking a sip of wine, I continue. "I moved to the city after I got my degree, and I've tried to avoid coming back this way."

"Is your dad still around? You must've come to visit him and your aunt and uncle. Did you come to visit them?" He matches my position and leans back against the back of the couch, relaxing into it.

"Yeah, he's around. His new wife is all right, but we butt heads a bit so I avoid coming around. I see him for the big holidays and we email on occasion. I saw Aunt Sheryl and Uncle Rob more often than Dad. They had a big part in raising me." I look down at my hands and take a shaky breath, trying to get my emotions in check. I watch him study me from the corner of my eyes before he changes the subject and the mood lightens once more.

The evening and bottles of wine wear on, and we are completely engrossed in talking to one another that I don't even notice the time. "Shit, Jack, it's well past midnight. We've been talking for almost four hours. I need to get to bed!"

"Yeah, I should probably go as well." He stands and sways in his spot, a little drunk from the amount of wine consumed.

"You're not going anywhere. You're too drunk. I'll sleep on the couch since I'm smaller, and you can take the bed."

"No, I don't want to impose. I'll be okay. I'm not that far from home anyway."

"Jack, I don't know your middle name, Madison, you *aren't* driving. I don't have to get up early for work tomorrow, so you can buy me breakfast or something to make up for it. Get your ass into that bedroom and go sleep the wine off." I point toward the bedroom and hold my ground.

"It's Benjamin, and honestly, it's not a big deal." He tries moving toward the door to leave, and I feel my heart racing. Memories of my mom flood my mind.

In a panic, I blurt out, "My mom was killed because of a drunk driver. Please don't do this. Please don't leave." My vision goes blurry as tears start falling down my cheeks. He stops in his tracks and turns to look at me, surprise written on his face.

"I'm so sorry, Kaylan." He pulls me into a warm embrace, and I bury my face in his chest, the tears falling from my eyes staining his shirt. He is warm and puts me at ease, stroking his hand up and down my back in a soothing motion. His muscles tense and relax under my touch, and I don't want to let go. "Shh," he says as I start crying a little harder into him, my grip tightening on him. "I'll stay, I promise. I won't leave tonight." He gives the top of my head a small kiss, and I nod my head in understanding before pulling back to look him in the eyes. His own reveal guilt.

"Sorry, I didn't mean to become a blubbering mess. Wine tends to make me more emotional than normal, and I don't want to see you or anyone else get hurt because of something that could have been avoided." I sniff and wipe my eyes on my t-shirt, trying to get ahold of my emotions. "There were some clothes that were in the drawers when I got here. I'm sure something will fit you. They are in the closet. Come on." I wave at him to follow me down the hall.

I dig through the closet and pull the clothes out and hand them to him. "I think they might have been my uncle's or something. They were here when I moved in." Jack takes the clothes and mumbles his thanks. He pulls his shirt over his head, exposing a beautifully chiseled body. He has a little bit of light brown chest hair and some around his navel; I can't help but stare at his perfect physique. I lick my lips, imagining what he looks like without his pants on, and I have to shake my head to rid it of those thoughts.

"Sorry, I ah, I didn't mean to stare." I turn my back to him, trying to calm myself. He laughs, and it's a deep, husky chuckle. I can hear the rustling of clothes as he finishes changing. I close my eyes and press my legs tighter together, willing the warm feelings in my stomach and between my legs to go away.

"You can turn around now. I'm covered up." I turn around again so I can look into his beautiful eyes. "We can share the bed if you want. I can sleep on top of the covers, or I can take the couch." He takes a small step forward, and I automatically take one back.

"No, I don't think that's a great idea. Kevin..." I trail off.

"Yes, Kevin. Sorry. I didn't even think of that; I just didn't want to kick you out of your bed since this is your place. That's all. I swear I didn't mean anything else by it." He holds up his hands, palms facing me in surrender.

"Right, no, totally. I didn't think you meant anything by it. I'll be fine on the couch. Goodnight, Jack." I grab a pillow and make my way back into the living room, closing the door behind me. I sit down on the couch, place my head in my hands, and let out a small groan. *What am I doing?* I push out a harsh breath, turn off the light, and try to get as comfortable as I can, willing sleep to pull me under.

After tossing and turning for what feels like hours, my mind stops running long enough to sleep, but it is anything but peaceful. I wake a few hours later with images of Jack running through my mind. I look at the clock on the stove and see it's six in the morning. *Great.* I get up, my mouth dry from all the wine, and grab a glass to fill with water before I turn on the coffee maker, trying to be quiet to not disturb Jack, whom I figure is still fast asleep.

I turn on the lamp by the couch and pick up my book, deciding to read a bit while I wait for him to wake up. About thirty minutes later, he comes out of the bedroom, fully dressed, and pauses when he sees I'm awake. I must have startled him because he looks guilty.

I smile up at him; he looks great in the mornings. His chin has a fair amount of stubble on it, and his hair is messy but suits him. "Morning, Jack. Attempting the walk of shame?"

He smirks at the comment. "Can't do the walk of shame. We didn't do anything. You wouldn't even share the bed with me so you could get a decent amount of sleep."

"Eh, the couch was fine. My body is getting used to being up this early because I'm usually down in the shop by now baking up a storm. Want some coffee?"

He nods his head. "That would be great, thanks, just cream." He takes a seat on the couch and spreads out. I bring the mug back into the living room and hand it to him, happily taking a sip of my own.

"I have to ask since you come into the shop almost every day for an éclair. How much do you work out to maintain those abs? They are impressive, I must say."

He snorts as he takes a sip of his coffee, almost spilling it on himself, and blushes. "I work out enough to allow me to eat your delicious pastries, but I don't know if I could tell you how much. A few hours a week I guess."

"Hmm, well if I could look like that and still eat sweets, I would in a heartbeat."

"You look great. Don't say that."

"You didn't see me before; otherwise, you wouldn't say that," I murmur and play with the hem of my shirt.

"Sure, I have. That's you in the picture in the bedroom, isn't it?" I groan and try to hide my face as I nod my head. "If that's how you looked then, I think you look great. You're happy in that picture. You look content. If we are going to be friends, you're not going to put yourself down. Got it?"

"Sure," I say, trying my best to appease him.

"I call bullshit on your *sure*," he says, making air quotes. "I'm serious. I've worked hard to remove negative things from my life. I don't want my friends going down the same route I did."

"Okay, deal. I won't say anything."

"Great. Well, the coffee is good, but I did promise you breakfast and I know a great spot around the corner that's open. Get on some clothes and we'll go. My treat." His smile is infectious, and I can't help but agree to food. Getting up off the couch, I head to my bedroom to change. I stop in the entryway. He made the bed and folded the clothes I gave to him to sleep in. It is such a small gesture, but it is so kind and unexpected that my heart gives a little leap. *Maybe becoming friends with him is a bad idea?*

I shake the thought from my head. Men and women can be friends and nothing more; there is no reason why *we* can't, too. I'm in a happy relationship, and Jack is just a friend in town. Nothing more. I change quickly, emerging in a pair of skinny jeans, a fitted purple t-shirt, and boat shoes. I watch Jack appraise my outfit and he gives a slight nod.

"Ready?"

"Yup, am I driving, or are you?"

"It's close enough, I figure we can walk. If that's okay with you?" I nod and we head downstairs and out onto the street. Our conversation is casual. His fingers keep brushing against mine as we walk, and I yearn to hold his hand. I grumble to myself as we walk inside the diner. He holds the door open and ushers me in first.

"Hey, Steph." Jack waves to the aging waitress upon entering.

"Jack, how are you, sweetie?" she asks, coming over and giving him a small peck on the cheek. "Who's this lovely lady, hm?" She elbows him in the stomach. I watch when he flinches a tiny bit before introducing me. "This is my friend, Kaylan. She's Sheryl's niece and the new owner of *The Sweet Shoppe*. Kaylan, this is Steph, a good friend of the family's"

"It's a pleasure to meet you." I extend my hand to shake hers.

"Oh, Jack, good job with this one. She's got manners, unlike that last girl. What was her name? Muriel? Matilda?"

He laughs, but I can tell it's not a genuine one. "It was Monica," he mumbles.

"Well, whoever she was, she wasn't right for you. This girl here seems much better for you."

Now, it's my turn to be embarrassed. "We're just friends. I have a boyfriend."

I see the moment she realizes her faux pas, and she shakes her head to clear her thoughts. "I'm sorry, I just figured because it is so early in the morning. Where are *my* manners? It's nice to meet you, Kaylan. I didn't mean to imply."

"It's all right, Steph. I'm new to town, and I don't have a lot of friends so Jack has volunteered for the job." I smile, leaning into him and knocking him with my shoulder. "He tells me this is the best place for breakfast, so here we are."

She shows us to a table and takes our orders. When I try to order just a bowl of oatmeal, Jack scoffs and insists I order pancakes as they were the best he's ever had. I cave and order them with blueberries and a side of fruit instead of the hash browns. I'm digging in when my phone goes off. Scrambling to pull it out of my pocket, I drop it and swear under my breath. I look at the caller ID and see it's Kevin.

"Shit, I have to get this. Be right back," I excuse myself and head for the front door, answering the call before it goes to voicemail.

"Hey, Kev. Good morning."

"Hey, hun, I wanted to check in to see how you're doing."

"Fine, I'm at breakfast right now." I look in through the window and see Jack, talking with Steph, and I catch myself smiling.

"By yourself?"

"Uh, no, I'm with Uncle Rob." I bite my lip as the lie passes through. It's not that I want to lie to him, but I don't think it would be best to admit I'm out with Jack, even though it's just as friends. "Oh, listen, I found out who owns *Red Bird*. It's Jack. I'm going to ask him to give you a call."

"Oh," he pauses. "Jack, huh?" Another pause. "Okay, yeah, have him call me. Listen, not to change the subject, but I wanted to let you know I'm going out of town for business. I'm leaving Wednesday and will be gone for almost two weeks, so I won't be able to get out there to see you. I wanted to know if there was a chance you could come by here today or tomorrow."

"Oh, Kev, that's great news, but I won't be able to get out there. I have a ton of work I need to get done today, and then I'm at the bakery all day the next few days. I'm really sorry."

"Oh, yeah. No, I get it. It's fine."

"Please don't be mad at me. I'm swamped over here. Plus, I have a meeting with Dan tonight to go over the business and where we stand with everything."

"I get it. It's all right. I just hoped I could see you before I left. It's going to be a lonely week and a half." He pouts, and I chuckle.

49

"I'll make up for it when you're back, I promise."

"Good. Well, good luck with work and Dan. Don't go too crazy over there."

"Thanks, I'll talk to you later." When I hang up the phone, relief washes over me. I walk back into the diner and plop down in my seat, taking a giant bite of my pancakes. I moan quietly as the tart blueberries and sweet syrup run over my taste buds. I swallow and cut another piece. "These are so good, Jack."

"I told you they were the best," he replies, taking a strawberry from my fruit bowl and popping it in his mouth, winking at me.

"If you're stealing my fruit, you better be willing to share some of those home fries." I point the fork at him, and he pushes the plate closer to me.

"I thought you didn't want the potatoes. That's why you went for fruit."

"I didn't want a plateful. Doesn't mean I don't want a few though." I stab my fork through two of them and promptly pop them in my mouth. "Oh, God, these are so good," I moan loudly.

"Careful there, people are going to start asking for what you're having if you can't keep it down."

I smile and sarcastically respond, "Ha-ha. You should have been a comedian, Jack." Just to be a jerk, I take another bite of pancakes and moan loudly as I chew, closing my eyes in the process. I waggle my eyebrows at him when I open my eyes. He licks his lips and shifts in his seat. "I'm making you uncomfortable, aren't I?"

He clears his throat. "No, I'm fine." He smiles and looks down at his plate to concentrate on his food.

Changing the subject, I ask, "So, tell me a bit about how you got into the restaurant business."

I watch his face light up as he turns his attention back to me. "Oliver is an amazing chef. He went to school for it, of course, and I just happened to get lucky to become his roommate. He put an ad on Craigslist and I answered it. I had finished my degree in Business with a minor in Finance and was working for a small company that treated me like shit." He chuckles at the memory before continuing. "I knew I had to get out of there. Oliver had been working on new recipes for a month when I decided to start putting together a business plan for a restaurant.

"Four years later, here we are. We finally have a successful business, but it wasn't easy. We opened once before in the same spot, and it was a total flop. Oliver had to take a job at another restaurant to help pay back the loan, and I had to find a job. I worked a few odd jobs here and there; landscaping, repairman, et cetera." He takes a sip of coffee as he finishes his story.

"Wow, that's crazy! I'm glad things are working out well for you. You're a nice guy and you deserve happiness."

"Thanks, what about you? What's your real job?"

"Oh." I laugh. "Boring, that's what it is." I hold my coffee cup to my lips and peer at him over the mug.

He motions for me to continue. "Come on, I told you my tragic story, you could at least indulge me."

I push a heavy sigh past my lips. "Fine. I'm a Data Solutions Analytics Consultant." I pick up my fork, stab a grape, and put it in my mouth, chewing slowly.

"Wow, that's a long title. So, what does a Data Solutions Analytics Consultant actually do?"

"Healthcare solutions. Basically, I'm IT. It's very boring, but it pays a lot and allows me a decent apartment in the city, so I'm not going to complain *too* much."

"Ah, yes, the city. Tell me how you met Kevin. He seems," he takes a moment, "nice."

"He *is* nice, just stressed lately. This is a huge change for us and we are both trying to figure it out. I think I'm coping a bit better than he is though. He doesn't do small towns. It brings back bad memories of his childhood. That's why he's so weird when he's out here."

Looking at the time on my phone, I see we've been at the diner for a little more than an hour and I need to get some work done. "This has been great. I appreciate it. I do have to get back, though, and get some work done."

He studies my face as if committing it to memory before getting Steph's attention for the check. He leaves cash on the table and the two of us make our way out of the diner and toward my apartment.

"Thank you for breakfast. It was very nice of you." Our hands bump together as we walk and I pull away, crossing my arms over my chest.

"Thanks for joining me, and thanks for letting me crash at your place last night. You're right, it was best that I didn't drive last night. I'd had one too many."

"Anytime you need a place to crash, you're welcome to come over," I say, blushing, and rub my cheek to try and hide the color from him. His laugh is smooth and husky at the same time. It makes me want to say or do anything to hear it again.

Stopping in front of my apartment, he turns to look at me. "I'll keep that in mind. Good luck with work today."

"Thanks. Oh, give me your phone." I hold my hand out, waiting. Pulling the phone from his pocket, he places it in my hand and I open a text message to send one to myself. "Now you have my number, and I added Kevin's into your contacts. Please call him about the restaurant, or have Oliver call him. He usually doesn't get excited over food like this."

"Yeah, one of us will give him a call. See ya later." He takes his phone from my outstretched hand and walks toward his waiting Jeep. I watch him hop in and pull out, giving a small wave and smile as he drives out of view. The last thing I want to do is go upstairs to work. The thought is dreadful, and if I am being honest, I want to head to the shop to bake. *I blame you, Aunt Sheryl.* I think, making my way upstairs to begin work.

The emails and requests are nonstop, and I am beginning to wonder why I agreed to work like this. FMLA would probably have kicked in if I asked for it, but I figured I wouldn't be here for long. I've only been here for a week, though, and I'm already starting to wish I was staying long term. After answering the fifteenth email regarding the same issue for a different account, I decide to take a break and go for a walk. It is a beautiful day outside, and I don't want to waste it indoors.

I change into a pair of shorts and sneakers and head out into the mid-morning sun. I close my eyes and tilt my head back, the warmth on my face bringing an instant smile to my face. Behind my eyelids, I see the light dance as it filters through the leaves in the trees and it reminds me of my carefree days of summer. Just from stepping outside, I feel more relaxed.

I walk up the quiet sidewalk through the center of town, passing the closed businesses. Sunday still means something in a small town, and most shops are closed today or will only open for a few hours in the early afternoon. The exceptions are the few chain shops that have taken up residence in the actual center of town. Those are open seven days a week.

The park is still rather empty, and I take a seat on a bench that overlooks the small river. The sun is glistening off the soft white peaks that form as the wind blows over it gently. The bench is half-shaded from the large oak tree that stands next to it. I hear birds chirping and watch two blue jays chase each other squawking. I decide she is probably mad at him for doing something stupid, and I shake my head at the foolishness before closing my eyes to let my body relax.

I hear kids running around behind me, and I turn to watch their game of tag as their mother unpacks the picnic basket and puts the food out on the table. Her husband comes up behind her and wraps his arms around her waist, planting a gentle kiss on her cheek. The gesture is so loving and makes me happy. I start smiling like a goof. I pull my phone out from my pocket and open a new text message to Kevin.

Me: *I miss you and wanted to know if you're free to talk for a bit. I'm tired of working and need a break.*

I hold my phone in my hand, looking around waiting for a reply. After waiting for a few minutes and not hearing back, I call, but it's sent straight to voicemail. *That would explain why he didn't respond.* It's strange though; he always keeps it charged. It's his lifeline and he uses it for work. I try again, and it goes straight to voicemail again. Resigning myself to the fact I won't be able to talk to him now, I leave my spot and decide to head back.

Dinner is at Uncle Rob's house tonight, and I decide I want to bake something to bring for dessert. I make my way into the shop, passing others that were out enjoying the nice summer sun and air. Stopping in front of the shop, I dig the keys from my pocket and step inside, the rush of cool air feeling nice against my sticky skin.

I walk into the kitchen and grab the recipe box, looking for something to bake. I pass recipes for cookies, whoopie pies, cake balls, and cream puffs. Nothing seems to stick out to me. I want something that will be easy but still taste amazing, and I wish I knew what Uncle Rob's favorite thing was so I could make that. I pull all the recipes out of the box, determined to find the perfect thing, when I notice a small folded paper at the bottom of the box. I pull it out and gently unfold it, not wanting to damage the delicate looking parchment.

Bread Pudding. I study the recipe and the familiar hand-writing and smile; it's my mom's handwriting. This was one of her recipes and will be perfect. I wipe a stray tear from my cheek, not wanting to stain the recipe, and smile as I read over it a few times. I take a picture of the recipe and put everything back. Adding the ingredients to a list on my phone, I run to the grocery store to get the required items. I load up a basket with the only items I didn't already have in my apartment—condensed milk, bread, raisins, and nutmeg.

After carrying the few items up into my apartment, I get started right away. I take several slices of bread out of the packaging and cut it into chunks, measuring out three cups and pushing the measured amount to the side of the cutting board. I pop a leftover piece in my mouth and savor the flavor of the white bread, moaning a little as I chew it. I whip the eggs, condensed milk, sugar, and vanilla in a bowl before transferring it into a glass baking dish. I drop a few raisins in the dish then press the bread into the egg mixture, sprinkling more raisins and nutmeg on top.

I smile to myself and take a picture to send to Kevin before placing the entire thing in a preheated oven. It has been years since I've eaten bread pudding, and I hope I can cook it as well as my mom did. I sit on the couch and picture her baking it when I was little. She would let me help cut the bread and whisk the eggs and sugar together. We saved it for the rare occasions the loaf of bread was starting to go stale.

The aroma of the nutmeg and custard fills the kitchen, and I inhale deeply, a smile spreading across my lips as I let the breath out through my nose. It smells just like I remember it, like happy memories and love. I need someone to talk to, so I try Kevin again, but the phone goes straight to voicemail. I hang up and I dial Jack's number. He picks up on the second ring.

"To what do I owe the pleasure of a call?" he asks, clearly smiling.

"I'm making bread pudding, and I'm feeling nostalgic and need someone to talk to. I tried Kevin, but it's going straight to voicemail, so I figured if you had a few minutes I would bug you. Are you busy?"

I can hear him shuffling some stuff around and then after the distinct sound of a door closing, the background noise disappears. "I'm at the restaurant right now, just getting some paperwork done and supplies ordered, but I have a few minutes."

"Oh, sorry, I didn't even think! Most places are closed today so I assumed you guys were, too. I don't want to hold you up. You can get back to work." I'm trying to push him off the phone, not wanting to disrupt him further.

"Kaylan, it's fine. If I was too busy, I would have let it go to voicemail. Tell me about this delicious sounding bread pudding." His voice is smooth and calming. Every time he talks, he seems so relaxed; I wish I could be that way.

"How do you do it?"

"How do I do what?" he asks, confused. "Make bread pudding?"

I laugh. "No. Sound so relaxed every time we talk. I wish I could be as easy going as you."

"Oh, good, I was going to direct your question to Oliver, because I have no idea how to make bread pudding." He laughs before continuing. "I don't know, you put me at ease. I enjoy speaking with you. So, this pudding?"

I smile. "I found it with my aunt's recipes at the bottom of the box. It's one of my mom's, was in her handwriting. I used to make it on occasion with her, and it smells just like a remember it. It reminds me of my childhood."

"That's really nice. I'm glad it's making you happy. I know you have a lot going on, so I'm glad you found something to help relax for today." The phone goes silent, but I can hear his breathing on the other end. "Are you planning on eating it alone, or are you bringing it somewhere?"

"I'm going to dinner at my uncle's tonight, to meet with Dan, the bakery's accountant, so I wanted to bring dessert. When I saw this, I knew it's what I had to make. It just felt right."

"Then I'm glad you made it. Listen, I should get going now, but I'm glad you called. If you need help eating those leftovers, I'd be more than happy to take it off your hands."

"Of course, you would. You could eat anything and never gain a pound," I tease. "I'll make sure to save you some though."

His laugh is infectious and I chuckle with him. "I told you, I have to work out to look this good, but I look forward to tasting some of it. Thank you."

"Thanks for listening to me. Good luck at work. I'll see you later."

"Bye, Kay," he says as I hear the phone click and the line goes silent. *Kay.* No one has called me that since elementary school, when everyone's name got shortened because we were all too lazy to pronounce the syllables. It sounds nice rolling off his tongue. I think I like it. I shrug to myself and dial Kevin's number again, hoping to get him on the line this time. The phone rings, and rings, and rings. Finally, voicemail picks it up. I decide to leave a message.

"Hey, hun, I tried calling you earlier, and I texted you. Why was your phone off? That's not like you. Anyway, please call me. Love you." I hang up the phone and check the timer on the oven. The pudding still has twenty minutes until it's done, and I decide I need to try to focus on a little more work. Otherwise, Karen won't be happy.

My mind keeps drifting back and forth between focusing on my job, the bakery, Kevin, and Jack. Whenever it drifts to Jack, I linger there. I realize I'm doing it, and I shrink into myself, feeling horrible for thinking of Jack like that. I'm mentally cheating on Kevin. I've known Jack for a week, and I'm already thinking of him more than Kevin. *Fuck.*

CHAPTER SEVEN

*W*hen I arrive, I carry the bread pudding in, and Uncle Rob smiles.

"Don't tell me you bought that, too?" he teases.

"Nope, I made it all by myself. I found the recipe in Aunt Sheryl's stuff, but it was written in Mom's handwriting. I wanted to bring something tonight, and I thought this would be perfect."

His smile widens as he takes it from me to put in the fridge. "It will be great. Thanks for bringing it by."

We gather around the table and start a friendly conversation as the food is passed around the table.

"How's the shop been, Kaylan?" Dan asks, dunking his bread in the pasta sauce on his plate.

"It's been going fine. Denise and Jessica have been extremely friendly and helpful. Denise sure knows her way around the kitchen there, huh?" I take a bite of my pasta and chew slowly, waiting for him to reply.

"Yes, Denise has been there for a long time. She knows the ins and outs of that place. She's a good lady."

"Dan, can you tell me where we stand with the business? Are

we in good shape? Is there anything I need to be concerned about or need to do?"

He glances up from his plate to me and gives a small smile. "Let's finish dinner and then we'll talk about the business, hm?"

Shit. My mind is going a thousand miles an hour. Why doesn't he want to talk about it at dinner? Is the business in trouble? Every possible scenario begins running through my brain and I zone out. I do my best to act as if I'm in the conversation, nodding my head and humming occasionally as Dan and Uncle Rob talk. Finally, when I think I'll bust, Dan asks if we can speak in the living room. Uncle Rob agrees to handle the dishes while we go over things.

Dessert is brought out to us, and I murmur thanks to Uncle Rob and place it on the table, my stomach doing flips already. I give a nervous smile and take a seat on the couch; Dan is sitting next to me and placing his laptop on the coffee table. He opens the screen and pulls up a spreadsheet with hundreds of numbers on it. I'm getting dizzy looking at all of them.

"Okay, do you have any knowledge about income statements?" My face gives him his answer, and he offers a kind smile in return. "That's all right. I'll walk you through it. This row here," he points to a row marked *revenue*, "is the amount that you bring it. This information gets pulled from the register. On Saturday nights, I get a list of the items that were sold for the week, and I add the totals for each week to the row."

I nod my head in understanding. He points to another row marked *expenses*. "This row is your monthly expenses. You have rent for the space, the small business loan from the bank, employee paychecks, health benefits, electricity, ovens, supplies, et cetera."

"Are the ovens and mixers and such just on loan? Do we not own them?"

"No, they were purchased. The bakery owns them. Sheryl

determined the life of the appliance and the amount it costs gets expensed over the course of its life. An example—Sheryl bought a new oven eight years ago, and she said it should last at least ten years. I figured out the monthly expense over five years, and if it lasts longer than that, it increases the net income because it does not have to be replaced as soon as anticipated. Does that make sense?"

I move my hand side to side in a rocking motion. "Kind of. Please continue."

"The numbers aren't looking horrible right now, but this also includes you not getting a paycheck, and the shop was closed for a week when she passed away. If we can't drum up more business within the next month, these numbers are going to get a lot tighter than I like to see. It's going to eat into some of the profits that we have set aside."

I groan quietly to myself. "So, if we stay on this current trajectory, how long before we are in trouble? What do I have to do to be able to get us on the right track?"

He stays quiet before answering. "We are looking at three months, tops. The only way I see this turning around is by selling more stuff, raising your prices, or letting someone go."

"I can't do that, Dan. What would Aunt Sheryl do?" I twirl the edge of my t-shirt, nervous as to his answer.

"I think she would find a way to sell more. She was too stubborn to let the place go downhill without a fight. I know you'll figure it out, too." He smiles at me as he eats some of his dessert. "This is delicious. You made it?"

I pick up my own bowl and smile shyly. "Yeah, found it in Aunt Sheryl's box of recipes."

"Well, if this is an indicator of your ability to bake, I think you're off to a great start. Remember, Rome wasn't built in a day."

We sit in silence, eating our dessert, when Uncle Rob comes out to join us. "Get everything you need?"

"I've got a starting point," I respond, looking up at him. Turning my attention back to Dan, I ask, "Is this information anywhere that I can access it easily? I want to be able to look at it and monitor it."

"Yes, I have it set up online. I can send you the link. Just create a login and then you can keep up with it."

"Perfect, thanks so much for all the help. I appreciate it."

He smiles warmly. "Just doing my job."

I make it back to my apartment, Uncle Rob insisting I take the leftovers with me so I don't have to cook anything. I feel bad for taking them but grateful that I won't have to cook for the next several days. I'm also looking forward to eating more bread pudding. I outdid myself for sure.

My phone begins ringing and I look at the caller ID. It's Kevin. I answer it quickly, not wanting it to go to voicemail.

"Kev, why was your phone off? I've been worried," I say.

"Sorry, phone was going to die, and I forgot the charger so I turned it off. I wasn't expecting calls from clients anyway so I figured it was no big deal. Sorry I worried you."

"It's fine. I got together with Dan, the accountant, today. It's not looking too good." I sigh.

"Why? What's wrong?"

"Our profits aren't as high as they should be. We aren't taking in as much. Soon, we are going to be going into the reserve. My brain is spinning trying to think of what I can do."

"How about you sell the shop so you don't have to worry about it?"

"That's a terrible suggestion. I want to at least give it a good try, see if I can do this. Honestly, I'm enjoying it. Life is less chaotic here, and baking is kind of fun." My tone lets him know I'm annoyed.

He huffs, and I know he is shaking his head at me. "Kaylan, you realize we have been at each other's throats since you left to go there? It's only been a week and it's like I can't say or do anything right. What's going on?"

I bite my lip. I've been annoyed with him lately. Taking a moment to gather my thoughts, I finally let out a deep breath. "It's the small comments you've been making to me. When I was sitting with Jack and the éclair was in front of me, you asked if I should *really* be eating that, or when I spent my morning baking, you told me to be careful and not eat too many treats. What's with the comments?"

"We've been over this. I know how hard you worked to lose the extra weight you had, and I don't want to see you put it back on because you now work at the sugar shack. I've already told you that. I'm not trying to be an asshole, just realistic," he replies nonchalantly.

"That's really rude, Kev. It's not like I had a choice to do this. She left it to me. I didn't want to take over this place. I didn't want the responsibilities that a business brings. I didn't want to have to work two jobs and hardly sleep. I didn't ask for any of this, but I was forced into it." I'm fuming. The words are tumbling out of my mouth so quickly, I'm sure I'm mumbling everything. "Also, I never asked for you to understand or to help. I just asked that you stand by me and support me. I feel like that is the last thing I've gotten from you though. It's what I need from you right now, and you aren't even there for me."

I take a deep breath. My body is shaking, the adrenaline is running high, and I can hear my heartbeat in my ears.

"Maybe we should take a few days. I leave for my trip so let's just talk after that. Give you a chance to calm down and we can circle back, okay?" he asks, annoyance dripping from his voice.

"Awesome, you just want to avoid it. You know what, Kev, fine. I'll talk to you when you're back. Good luck." I hang up the phone quickly, not even giving him a chance to respond, and toss it on the couch. I grab a pillow and bury my face in it to muffle the blood-curdling scream I let out. I'm angry, I'm hurt, and I'm *pissed*! When my phone rings, I assume it's Kevin, and I yell into the receiver. "What? Circling back already?"

"Oh, um, sorry. Kaylan?" Jack asks, his voice timid.

I cover my mouth with my hand and drop my head in defeat, taking a deep breath. "I'm so sorry, Jack. Kevin and I had a fight, and I thought you were him. What's going on?"

"I wanted to find out how your bread pudding came out? You were so excited earlier, and I wanted to know if it lived up to your expectation?"

"If it's not too late, you can come over and have some; otherwise, I might eat it all myself."

"Only if you want the company. I'm leaving work in a few minutes." His voice is smooth and unwavering.

"Yeah, I probably shouldn't be left alone or I really *will* eat all of the pudding. You can't stay too late because I have work in the morning, but for a little while would be fine." I smile, thinking how sweet he is for checking up on me. "See you soon." I hang up the phone, change into pajamas, and pull the glass dish out of the fridge with two spoons. The thought of wine crosses my mind, but I decide against it. It's better to not drink when I'm upset.

The buzzer downstairs goes off, and I stick a spoonful of pudding into my mouth before I get up to allow him in. I stand by the door, waiting, my spoon hanging from my mouth. I pull it out and open the door when I hear the faint knock, not even acknowledging him before I take a seat back on the couch and pull the pudding into my lap.

"Wow, it must have been bad if you're sitting there with all the pudding to yourself. Move over." He pushes my knee and I scoot over, allowing him room to sit as I hand him a clean spoon. "Wanna talk about it?"

"He's being an asshole, so no. I invited you over so I didn't eat all this myself, remember?" I take another spoonful and place it in my mouth. He reaches over into the dish and scoops some out for himself, placing the sweet treat in his mouth.

"Damn, this is awesome. You made this?" he asks, grabbing more and shoving it into his mouth greedily. I smile and snort through my nose, watching the faces he's making. He closes his eyes and tilts his head back before his lips push up into a huge grin.

"You like it?"

"I love it. I would consider this up there with the éclairs I buy every day. Great job, Kaylan," he praises.

I duck my head and smile. "Thanks. I'm happy with how it came out, too." I place another spoonful in my mouth and then place the dish on the coffee table. I let out a deep, steadying breath before I continue. "The shop isn't doing well. I was trying to talk to Kevin about it, and he wants me to sell it and come back to the city."

"Is there anything I can do to help?" He turns his body so he is facing me head on, really listening to my answer.

I shake my head no. "Unless you can magically make it so I have more sales. I couldn't ask you to do anything, and I don't mean for you to start buying more éclairs either." I laugh quietly. "No, I need to figure this out. It's okay, I have about a month to sort things out before Dan said he was going to be concerned. That's very sweet of you though." I place my hand on his knee, not wanting to make eye contact.

This is how Kevin should have reacted. He should have been offering to help make this better, not talking me into giving up so quickly. I'm lost in my head, my annoyance and hurt by Kevin's comments running my emotions, and I feel my eyes well up with tears. I feel like I don't know him anymore. He used to push me and support me in every aspect, but this? He is acting as if he wants me to fail.

"Hey, what's wrong? Why are you crying? Did I say something to upset you?" He sticks his index finger under my chin and tilts my head up to look him in the eyes. I quickly wipe the tears away and take a calming breath.

"No, it's fine, I'm being stupid. I think it's all the sugar I've had. I already had some of this today, and then with the pancakes this morning. My body is probably freaking out."

He appraises me, and I feel my cheeks flush under his gaze. I'm not sure if he believes me, but he lets it slide anyway, opting to pick up the dish and eat more.

"You're gonna finish the rest of that, aren't you?" I ask, making a go for the pudding with my spoon.

He pulls it away from me and cradles it like he's trying to keep a ball from a rival teammate. "You said you were done. This is mine now."

I dive toward him, trying to pry the pudding from his hands. His body is so firm under my own, and I feel every muscle as he flexes and moves out of my grasp. He puts the dish down and starts tickling me, pushing me back the other direction. I'm shrieking and laughing so hard as his fingers find the hidden spots on my body. He pins me under him, the two of us laughing when I scream out, "Uncle! I give up!"

He stops tickling me but doesn't move. My body is still pinned under his, with his face only inches above mine. It's like we are in a bubble, completely frozen, time standing still. My body is zinging, and I'm hyper-aware of everything going on around me—the hitch in my breathing, the sudden intake of his breath, the heat rushing to my core, the twitch against my leg. I gaze into his lust-filled, blue eyes before a small moan escapes and I close my eyes, willing him his close the distance so I can feel his blush lips against mine.

He shifts and pulls his body off mine, helping me sit up in the process. "This isn't right, Kaylan. You're upset. You would regret it if we did anything." The four words he utters, *you would regret it,* bring time back with a crash. I blink at him a few times, embarrassment flooding my entire body.

"Oh, God, Jack, I'm so sorry." I put my hands up, palms out in surrender. "I'm making a fool of myself. I'm not that type of girl." I'm panicking.

His voice is calm and reassuring. He places a hand on my forearm, and I tense under his touch. "Kaylan, it's fine. You're upset and it was in the moment. I don't think any less of you. I know you didn't mean anything by it. It's forgotten. No harm done."

I drop my head in my hands, wanting to die from embarrassment. "Maybe you should go. I'm so sorry, I shouldn't have done that."

He gets up and walks toward the door. "Hey, don't think about it. It's fine. I'll see you tomorrow, okay?" he asks, his hand on the handle, waiting for my answer.

"Yeah, I'll see you tomorrow."

He walks out and closes the door quietly behind him. I groan and press my face into the nearest pillow and scream. *What am I doing?*

CHAPTER EIGHT

J'm in full swing in the kitchen, with flour on my cheek and chocolate on my fingers. I'm a hot mess, but I'm getting through the morning stuff—whoopie pies, éclairs, and cream puffs. Denise will be in soon, and I want to have as much done as I can so she doesn't have too much to do while I leave for a little while for work. I'm dancing around the kitchen, gathering ingredients to make the cake balls.

There is a loud crackling noise and then... nothing. It sounds like someone switched off a high voltage switch. Despite the radio going, the kitchen is eerily quiet. I walk over to the oven and look at the temperature gauge, watching it drop a degree. A minute later, it drops another. *No, no no! This is not happening!* I try turning the dial to turn up the temperature, but nothing. It keeps going down.

"Shit," I yell and wipe my forehead on my arm, trying to remain calm.

"Watch the language, missy," Denise says, pushing open the kitchen door and placing her hands on her hips. "What's so bad this early in the morning that has you swearing?"

67

"I think the oven just broke. I heard a loud crackling noise, and I've been watching the temperature go down."

"Hm, well that will suck, won't it?" she responds sarcastically. "How much do you have left to do?"

"I was getting ready to start the cake balls, but everything else is baked. We need to make the cream for the puffs and éclairs, the ganache, and the filling for the whoopie pies."

She opens her eyes wide and smiles. "You've been busy this morning, haven't you?"

I nod my head. "Yeah, I have to leave for a few hours to get my other job done, and I wanted to leave you with as few things to do if possible. Also, I didn't sleep well last night so I got an early start."

"Trouble in paradise?" She moves around the kitchen, grabbing the ingredients for the cream filling.

"Yeah, we had a fight. He's not being supportive of me running this bakery, and it's adding a lot of stress between us. Ugh, I don't know, Denise." I throw my hands up in defeat. "Maybe he's right."

She shrugs her shoulders and then turns to face me. "Let me ask you a question. Are you enjoying doing this, working in a bakery and putting smiles on people's faces?" Her eyes begin searching mine, looking for the answer.

The corners of my lips twitch into a small smile before I nod my head a fraction of an inch.

"Yeah, I am having fun doing this. It's nice being able to do stuff with my hands instead of type away on a computer and listen to people complain because the program isn't working correctly."

"Now, I'm not going to get involved in a lover's quarrel, *but* I think you should do what you're enjoying. If you fail, you fail, but you go down fighting. Don't give up because it's easy. No one ever said your aunt didn't work damn hard at this. She was here more hours than at home. We hired Jessica to give her some time to spend with Rob."

"I know, Denise, and you're right." I take a deep breath and smile. "Honestly, I haven't been this happy in a few years. It just seems right, being here. It feels like home."

She opens her arms, and I step into them for a big hug. "You are so much like her, Kaylan. I'm so happy she left you the bakery. I can't imagine anyone else owning it." She pulls back and holds me at arm's length to look at me. "You look so much like your mother. She was a good woman, just like your aunt. Both were taken too soon."

I feel my eyes begin to water. "You knew my mom?" My voice cracks on the word 'mom'.

"She used to help Sheryl out during busy times of the year so she was around a bit. The two of them would laugh so hard together that they would practically be in tears. It was always fun listening to them. You couldn't help but laugh with them when they would start." She reaches over and wipes a fallen tear from my cheek. "None of that now. We have an oven to get fixed and stuff to finish before everyone comes in. Does the oven in your apartment work? We could bake the cake up there for today."

I nod my head. "Yeah, it does. I'll bake this up there. Is it okay if I stay up there for the time being so I can get a little work done?"

"Yeah, that's fine. I'll finish this out." She shoos me away from her as she ties an apron around her ample waist.

"Thanks, Denise." I turn and walk out the door with the bowl of batter and a baking sheet.

I get everything upstairs and manage to unlock the door without spilling anything, and I am thankful for that. Placing the items on the counter, I turn on the oven to let it preheat. I look at my phone, hoping for a missed call or text from Kevin, but come up short. *Of course not,* I think, pouring the batter into the pan and putting it in the oven. After I get it baking, I take out my laptop to get some work done.

I'm so wrapped up in answering emails, I almost forget about the cake. "Shit," I yell, jumping up from my seat, hoping it isn't too burnt. I pull it out of the oven and look at it. Most of it seems to be salvageable; guess we'll just have fewer cake balls today. I place the sheet down on the cooling rack and begin thinking about what Dan said about how to get more money coming in.

The simplest solution is going to be raising the prices. Inflation happens all the time and people will still pay for it if it's good, *right?* I open a blank spreadsheet and list all the items we sell with the current prices, and also what I think it should be raised to. I look at it and smile. The increases aren't that much, but it is enough to start bringing in a little extra cash. I send it to Dan for him to take a look, and if he agrees, then we can get the registers updated to reflect the new prices.

Next on the agenda is finding someone to fix the oven. I wonder if Jack knows of someone, and I look at the clock to see it is seven-thirty. Praying he is awake, but not wanting to wake him up in case he isn't, I open a text message.

Me: *Hey, I didn't want to wake you, but it seems our oven died. Do you know of anyone that can fix it? If not, I'm just going to look up a repairman.*

A few minutes pass by, and someone is buzzing at the door downstairs. *Who the hell is that?* I get up and press the call button. "Can I help you?"

"Kay, it's me. Let me up." Jack's voice comes through the speaker and he sounds winded.

I hit the unlock button and let him up, and open the front door to let him in. He takes the stairs two at a time, and when he comes into view, I want to melt. He is in a pair of black basketball shorts and a fitted grey Under Armor t-shirt. His headphones are strung around his neck, and he smiles at me when he notices I'm watching him. He lifts up the bottom of his shirt to wipe the sweat from his brow, and it exposes his chiseled stomach. I stifle my moan and bite my lip, holding it in place.

He stands in front of me and pulls my bottom lip out from between my teeth with his thumb. "You're going to break skin if you bite that any harder," he says quietly.

"What are you doing here?" I ask, my voice coming out smaller than I mean it to.

"I was in the neighborhood for a run when I got your text. Thought I'd take a look and see if I can figure it out."

"Oh, that's nice of you. Thank you. I just need the cake to cool down a bit more before I go back with it. "Can I get you something? Food? Water? Shower?" My eyes widen a fraction when I realize I said the last bit out loud.

"Only if you're going to join me for the last one," he whispers and smiles seductively.

I pull my lip back between my teeth and bite it again, my face heating up from embarrassment.

"What did I tell you about that lip?" he asks, pulling it out from my teeth and rubbing the pad of his thumb along my lower lip, soothing it. Our eyes lock together and he starts leaning down, his lips inches from mine. I flutter my eyes closed and part my lips ever so slightly, waiting to feel his supple lips on mine. He drops his hand to my cheek and pulls me closer, our lips barely grazing one another's when my phone goes off. Just like that, the spell is broken.

I pop my eyes open and look at him, pulling away enough to put some distance between us. My phone continues to ring, and I reach out for it to answer without breaking eye contact with Jack. "Hello?" I ask, feeling the rapid rise and fall of my chest.

"Kaylan, it's Kevin." Those three words have reality crashing back to me, and I turn my back on Jack.

"Hi, Kevin. What's up?"

"I spent all night thinking about this, and I think, while you're there, it would be best to take some time apart from one another. Let you take the time you need to figure out what you want to do without me pressuring you into anything. I know you've been stressed lately, and this way I'm not adding to it. You can still come and go as you please to the apartment. I know you don't have an option right now. We can keep things how they are until things quiet down.

The words are leaving his lips, and my brain is only registering about half of them. "Why?" It is the only thing I can think to ask.

"I told you, I don't want to be an added stress for you right now. I think this will be good for the both of us. It will allow us each time to think and breathe, figure out what we really want."

"Who is she?" I ask, not believing his reason for the break-up.

I hear him sigh heavily. "There's no one else. It's just you, Kaylan. You've been stressed, and I've been stressed. We've practically been at each other's throats since you went out there a few weeks ago." I hear voices talking in the background. "Listen, I've gotta go. We'll talk more about this after I'm back from my business trip if you want. Later."

I hear the phone click off before I even get a chance to respond. "Bye," I say out loud to no one. I turn around to see Jack standing there solid as a rock, his jaw clenched and his hands in fists by his sides. He's staring at me, but I can't make eye contact with him so I look at the floor. "Gonna come down to the shop and look at that oven? The cake should be cooled enough that I can bring it down." I begin moving around the apartment, trying to do anything but think about the conversation.

"Kaylan," he says softly as I continue to ramble.

"I know Denise is gonna want help again. There is a lot to do in the shop."

"Kaylan," he repeats, louder this time. I turn to look at him, my vision blurring with unshed tears. This is the second time today I'm going to cry.

"What?"

"Talk to me. What happened? Is he cheating on you?"

"Sorry you had to hear any of that. You shouldn't have to deal with my problems, and I don't want to talk about it right now. Now, the oven?" I ask, trying to steer the conversation back to neutral ground. He nods his head, and the two of us make our way down to the shop.

"Denise," I call out as I walk back toward the kitchen. "Jack's here to help with the oven. He said he can take a look, might know what's going on." I place the baking sheet down on the counter and pull out a bowl to start tearing the cake up.

"Hi, Jack," she calls over her shoulder as she continues to stir the chocolate on the stove.

"Hi, Denise. Nice to see you."

"You too, hun. Been seeing you around here a lot lately. How come?"

I look up from my task and look at him, watching his face redden from the attention.

"Kaylan and I have become friends and I don't have many of those in town. Plus, where else can I get the best éclair in the whole world?" He smiles at me, and I look back down to my task as he gets to work, looking at the oven. He pulls it out from the wall and begins looking over the wires and hoses. The three of us work in comfortable silence, my mind drifting to the conversation with Kevin. I start squeezing the cake through my fingers as I worked out my aggression.

"Kaylan?" Jack calls out to me.

73

I shake my head and bring my attention back to him. "Sorry, spaced out there. Did you figure out what's wrong?"

He rubs the back of his neck, a look of concern on his face. "You're probably not going to like the answer." I give a tight smile and motion for him to continue. "It looks like it's the thermostat or possibly the fan. I don't know if one is related to the other, or if they are both dead though."

"Awesome, any idea how to fix them?" I ask, hopeful.

He shakes his head. "Not that easy of a fix. You're gonna have to call someone and have them come out to repair it."

"Again, awesome." I smack the bowl to push it away from me and wipe my hands on a towel. I watch Denise as I pass her on my way to the small back office, and she keeps looking back and forth between Jack and me like she's watching a tennis match. I can feel Jack's presence behind me as I start rummaging through the Rolodex, trying to do anything to keep my mind occupied.

He takes a small step closer, his hand reaching for my hip and his front side grazing my backside. "I can ask Oliver if he has the number for a repairman." I can feel his body heat through my thin clothes and it makes me dizzy. I can't think straight.

"What are we doing, Jack?" I ask as I stop looking for the number.

"I'm trying to help a friend in need," he responds quietly, his breath tickling my neck as he speaks.

"I don't mean the phone number," I say, turning around so I'm facing him. "Why me?" I ask, searching his eyes for an answer. He brings his hand to my cheek and starts rubbing small circles on it with the pad of his thumb, and he smiles sweetly.

"Why not you? You're beautiful and kind and funny. There aren't many girls like you, Kay, and any guy is a fool to let you go." His lips are on mine in an instant, soft and needy, while his beard scruff rubs deliciously against my soft skin. The spark between us is electric, and I don't remember feeling this with anyone before.

He coaxes my lips apart with his tongue, and I oblige, moaning into his touch. He pulls my body flush with his and twists his fingers in my hair. My hands are wrapped around his back, and I feel his muscles flex and relax under his thin shirt.

Finally, we pull apart, both breathless and needy. He places his forehead down on mine and moves his hands so he is cradling the sides of my head. I grab on to his forearms and we stay like this, breathing each other in, letting ourselves calm down. I lick my lips, needing to feel and taste him again, and I hear a small groan escape his mouth.

"You're intoxicating, Kaylan. You taste like the bakery—sugar and chocolate. I've wanted to do that since we met."

"Jack." My voice is breathy and needy. "Please kiss me again." I lean forward, trying to tempt him back. I don't care how needy it makes me sound; I need to taste him again. He is like a drug. I got a small taste and I need more to help quench the thirst.

"Not here, Kaylan, not while Denise is right out there. Let me take you out, or you can come over to my place and I'll cook."

I nod, not trusting my voice, and take a deep breath. "I'd like that a lot. I can bring the dessert if you want to cook, or you can take me out and we can come back for dessert. Whatever you want to do I'm fine with."

He smirks and drops his hands to his sides, my face now chilled without his warm embrace. "Perfect. How about we do a quiet evening in then? We can get to know one another and talk. If it's a nice night out, we can sit on the back porch with the fire pit going? How's that sound?"

It sounds like heaven and I'm picturing it all in my mind. "It sounds great. I'd like that a lot."

"Perfect, I'll pick you up at seven tonight. Is that all right?"

"Yeah, that's fine, but won't you be working tonight? I don't want to get in the way of your job."

He pulls me in and places a quick kiss on my lips. "That's

sweet, but one of the perks of being the boss is I can come and go as I please. It won't be a problem. Let me know if you can't find the number for a repairman, and I can get the information from Oliver for you."

"Okay, thank you, Jack. I appreciate the help." I watch him walk out of the office, and I peek around to corner to see him leave the kitchen before I step back into the kitchen.

"Missy, you have some explaining to do," Denise says, her back still to me.

"I don't know what you're talking about. He was helping me find the number for a repairman."

"Uh huh, and his lips happened to slip and fall on yours? Did you find the number?" she asks. I blush, thinking of the kiss we just shared moments ago, my mind wandering, and I smile at the thought. When I don't answer, she pipes up again. "That's what I thought. I hope he is as good as he looks, but you need to find that number. Get back in there and look."

I turn on my heel and leave her alone to stuff the cream puffs as I searched for the number in case Jack's guy can't make it. My phone buzzes in my pocket, and I light up the screen to find a text from Jack.

Jack: *I can't wait to taste those sweet lips of yours again, beautiful. See you in a bit when I come back for my éclair!*

A goofy grin crosses my face and I hit reply.

Me: *Thanks for helping to make my day a little brighter. I'll make sure to save you the best éclair I make today.*

I find the number for the repairman and glance at the clock. It's already eight in the morning, and the bakery is going open soon, so the repairman shop should be open by now. I dial the number, and on the third ring, an older sounding man answers. "Ted's repair."

"Hi, my name is Kaylan, and the oven over here at *Sweet Little Shoppe* is on the fritz. When would you be able to come and take a look at it?" I can hear him rustling through some papers, flipping through a calendar, I assume.

"I can't get there til' Wednesday afternoon."

"Wednesday?!" I practically yell at him. "There is nothing before that? I can't not bake for two more days."

"I've got a few appointments before yours. I'm sorry, but that's all I have, miss."

I think I might throw up. My earlier high with Jack is now gone, and a weight sits in the pit of my stomach instead. "Please put me down for it." We hang up the phone and I text Jack.

Me: *Can I get the number for your guy? The repairman I have can't get here until Wednesday to fix it.*

Jack: *Sure, I'll get it from Oliver. Don't worry, it will all work out. If you have to, I'm sure you can use the kitchen here in the morning.*

It's a kind gesture and I giggle. Kevin would never have offered something like that.

CHAPTER NINE

*T*he day at the bakery went as smooth as it could go without an oven. We sold out of practically everything, but Denise did make two trips to my apartment to bake some more cookies while I was working. Jack called in a favor to his repairman, and his guy is able to get to the shop tomorrow morning. He's going to bring the parts Jack said he thought might be broken. That way he can fix it quicker if needed. All in all, the day was a success.

I finish answering my last email and close my computer, glancing at the time on my phone. It is only five, which means I still have two hours before Jack is coming to get me. I did promise him dessert so I figure I will make something special for the two of us. My baking skills have improved immensely in the last two weeks, and I'm confident I can bake everything and anything in the shop.

I google search a recipe for brownies, opting for something on the easier side, and find one that doesn't seem too difficult. These brownies have a secret ingredient that makes me smile. *He won't expect this.* I get to work pulling the ingredients out, along with the bowls and measuring cups and spoons. I go on autopilot as I began mixing the oil and sugar. Once it's mixed thoroughly, I add the eggs one at a time, then the vanilla. Finally, I add the dry ingredients and mix it until no flour remains. I stick my finger in the batter to taste it and smile. *It tastes like brownies to me.*

I place them in the oven and clean up the mess, sticking everything in the dishwasher and wiping down the countertop. I look around the kitchen to make sure it is clean and head toward the bathroom to take a quick shower while they bake. I have thirty minutes before the timer is going to go off—plenty of time.

I step under the warm water and let the jet stream hit my back, relaxing my muscles. I picture Jack again and the kiss we shared from earlier, my hand sliding down my body to the apex of my legs. The more I think about his soft lips and his rough hands, the wetter I get. I rub my throbbing clit faster, working myself into a frenzy. I picture his lips on mine and fantasize what it would feel like to have his tongue where my fingers are. The sexual tension has been building for a few days, and it doesn't take long for me to get off. I sigh contently and finish washing up to get out of the shower.

I wrap the towel around me and check on the brownies. There is still ten minutes on the timer, but when I stick a toothpick in them, it comes out clean. I pull them out of the oven and place the dish on a cooling rack. I head back to my room and begin changing. While it is summer, the nights are still a little cooler, so I opt for a pastel pink fit and flare lace dress with a nude lining, a light brown skinny belt, and a navy three-quarter length sleeve sweater.

I blow dry my shoulder length blonde hair until it is slightly damp then add some sea spray for texture and to help give me the beach curl waves. I add a splash of make-up to my face—mascara, highlighting powder to the apples of my cheeks, and I fill in my eyebrows. I finish the look with a swipe of gloss on my lips for a bit of shine. Taking another look in the mirror, I smile, happy with the look. I hear the buzzer and jog to the front door to allow Jack up. I look at the clock on the stove and realize he is a little early. *Good thing I got ready when I did.*

Hearing the faint knock on the door, I take a deep breath and put a smile on my face before opening the door. He stands there looking amazing, per usual. He is in a pair of dark wash fitted jeans, a light blue button-down shirt, and a pair of dress shoes. I appraise his form, push out a shaky breath, and suck my bottom lip between my teeth. *Damn, he looks good in his clothes!*

He clears his throat. "What did I tell you about that lip?" he asks, pulling it out from my teeth with his thumb. "Can I come in?" He raises his eyebrows in question.

I blush, not even realizing he is still standing in the doorway, and move to the side. "Yes, please. Sorry."

He steps into the room, and the air is instantly charged. I want to pull him down to me, to taste him again, but I refrain and keep my hands glued to my sides, not trusting myself.

"It smells great in here. What did you bake?" He takes a step closer, and I notice after taking a small one closer to him in return, our bodies are only inches from one another.

"Brownies. I said I would bring dessert, so I whipped something up. There is a special ingredient in it and I think you'll like it."

"I'm sure I'll love them. You look beautiful, Kay. That color looks good on you." He pushes my hair over my shoulder and grasps my face, pulling me closer to him. He leans down and plants a kiss on my lips. My hands instinctively wrap around his body and began caressing his back. This kiss is not as needy as the one earlier today; it's more relaxed. He bites my bottom lip gently, and a moan escapes my mouth. He takes his time, knowing there is no one here watching. Finally, he pulls away and smiles down at me.

"What was that for?"

"I've been wanting to do that again since this morning. It took all I had in me not to kiss you again when you handed me my éclair and sat with me today."

"Maybe I was waiting for the same thing. You should have been bold enough to make the first move," I tease.

"I'll keep that in mind for tomorrow. Are you ready to go?" he asks, motioning toward the door.

"Yep, let me get my shoes and purse. Do you want to cover the brownies with some tin foil? It's in the drawer next to the sink. I'll be right back." I walk down the hall and gather my items, looking at myself one last time in the mirror and noting my flushed complexion and kiss-swollen lips. I wipe the smeared gloss from my chin and refresh it before dropping the gloss in my purse.

I step back into his view, and he gives a low whistle. " Are you sure you don't want to go out and show off that fancy dress? I would rather keep you to myself tonight, but if you prefer..." He trails off.

"Nope, you promised me a home cooked meal and a quiet night in. I can go change if you want?" I point my thumb over my shoulder and look behind me toward my room.

"God, no, you look perfect. It might be difficult for me to keep my hands off you though." He grins devilishly and pulls me back into his arms, planting a quick kiss on my cheek. He picks the brownies up from the table, and we head out into the street where his Jeep is parked on the other side. He clicks the unlock button on the remote and walks around the car to my side. After opening the door, he waits until I'm settled before closing it and getting in on his side.

"Wow, you open all doors for ladies, huh?" I ask, a smile on my face.

"Only for the pretty ones." He winks as he pulls out on the

street. We ride in comfortable silence, the only noise coming from the radio and traffic outside.

"This is the way to my uncle's house, too. What road do you live on?" I ask, looking around at the familiar neighborhood.

"I live on Manzanita Lane. I bought the house a few years ago, but I keep to myself mainly so I don't know too many neighbors."

"My uncle lives on Chestnut Road, so that's what, about two or three streets over?"

He smiles and nods his head. "Yeah, we're really close then."

He pulls into his driveway, and I get the first view of his house. It's a cute ranch style with a single car garage and a large picture window in front. The landscaping is minimal, but it suits the house. There's a little bit of grass and a small garden area with a few bushes. He comes around and opens my door again, helping me down to the ground.

"Thank you."

He clasps his hand around mine and leads me into the house. "Mind taking off your shoes?" I just had the floors redone not too long ago," he says sheepishly. I toe my shoes off and look around as I enter, my face beaming. "Let me give you the tour and then we can do dinner. Can I get you something to drink? I seem to remember you liking wine a whole lot."

I laugh and shake my head. "See what I mean by you should be a comedian, Jack?" I take a deep breath. "I'd love some wine though." He puts the brownies on the table, pulls the wine out of the fridge, opens it, and pour us both a glass. I take a small sip and hum my appreciation as the fruity taste hit my tongue. "This is great. Thank you."

"So, clearly, this is the kitchen."

"Yes, clearly," I respond and take another sip of my wine as we walk into the spacious living room with a couch, recliner, and large flat screen TV mounted to the wall. Looking around, I notice there aren't any family pictures, just random pictures and knickknacks one would find from a store. "Living room." He motions around him and I nod. We walk down a small hallway, passing a bathroom, and at the end of the hallway, there are two bedrooms.

He pushes open the door for one of them and there isn't much in it—a bed, and a dresser, and a few pieces of artwork hanging on the walls. Then he opens the door to the master room. My mouth must hit the floor because it's breathtaking. It looks like he had a personal designer come in just for this room. Clearly, this is where he spends most of his time, as the rest of the house does not compare. There are beautiful French doors at the back, which lead out on to a back patio, and the king-sized bed is massive, sitting in the middle of the room. There is a large chair in the corner next to a dresser and a beautiful area rug on the floor.

"Wow, this is something else, Jack." I spin around slowly, taking everything in, and walk toward the doors to look outside to the backyard. "No offense, but this room is *amazing* in comparison to the rest of the house. It looks so comfy, I just want to curl up and stay here." I laugh as he stands next to me, both of us looking outside. He wraps his arm around my waist and plants a small kiss on the top of my head.

My stomach begins rumbling and he chuckles. "I think you need some food. Do you want to eat inside or outside? I don't know if the mosquitos are out tonight, but we can try it if you want."

"Outside sounds great. Can I help bring stuff out?" I ask, looking up at him, smiling.

He pushes open the doors from his bedroom and leads me out to the small table. "Sure, how about we leave our glasses and you can help me with the plates. We have beef stir-fry for dinner. Hope that's okay?"

"It sounds great." I place my glass on the table and follow him into the kitchen. He loads two plates with rice and stir-fry and hands one plate to me with a fork, knife, and napkin all rolled together. I cock my eyebrow and look up at him. "Fancy. I can tell you work in a restaurant."

"Yeah, it's a lot easier to carry everything out like this." We make our way back to the table outside and take our seats opposite each other, the smell of soy sauce and ginger flooding my senses.

"Jack, this smells amazing. You made this?" I ask, taking a bite. The taste is just as heavenly as the smell.

He gives a nervous chuckle. "Would you be mad if I told you Oliver made it?" He scrunches his face and laughs again.

"Maybe I'm on a date with the wrong person then?" I tease him, taking another bite of food.

"You like my abs, baby. Oliver doesn't have these. He has a small gut."

"I like more than just your abs, but that definitely helps." I take a larger sip of my wine, the alcohol making me a little bolder. He tips the bottle, refilling my glass and then filling his.

"Oh yeah? Besides my muscular body, what is it you like about me?" He's being bold as well, and I'm loving it. The flirting, the chase—it's thrilling.

"I like the way your eyes light up when we are talking about something that makes you excited. I like the way you laugh. It's infectious. I like the way you are chivalrous, always seeming to want to help someone in need. I like the way you look and your beautiful blue eyes. I could stare at them for days." I take another large sip of the wine to steady my nerves. That's a big confession to someone I just kissed today.

"Wow," he says quietly, taking a sip of his own wine. "Kaylan, I..." He pauses, trying to think of the correct words. "Thank you. That's probably the nicest thing anyone has ever said to me."

"You must have had girlfriends who said stuff like this to you all the time. No way I'm your first."

"Not the first, but the first in a long time. People don't look at me like they used to." I nod my head in acknowledgment, but I don't fully understand what he means. I continue to eat, hoping the food will help ward off the buzz I'm feeling. "Can I tell you a secret?" he asks, the corner of his mouth turning up in a smile.

I lean forward in my chair to listen. "I'm all ears."

"Kevin was a fool to let you go so easily. I'm not saying let's rush into anything, but I'd love to get to know you better and see where this goes. If you'll let me, that is."

I feel my cheeks heat up. "I'd like to get to know you as well, but I'm not ready to rush into this either. If we can keep it casual for now, I think that would be best."

"No pressure, promise." He reaches his hand across the table and cradles mine in his, rubbing his thumb along the side of my hand. I look at our hands and then back up to his face, cocking my head to the side to study him in the dim light. I smile and bite the corner of my lip, having an internal battle. I keep picturing what it would be like to run my tongue along his freshly shaved jaw and run my hands down the sides of his perfect body.

His eyes darken as he watches me. I notice the change and feel heat pool between my legs. "What are you thinking about, Kaylan?" His voice is deep and husky, sending a chill down my spine.

The alcohol making me brave, I decide to tell him the truth. "I'm wondering what it would be like to lick your perfect jaw and run my hands down your muscular body." He gulps and licks his lips while pushing his chair back from the table, allowing me access to sit on his lap if I so choose.

"Why don't you come over and find out?" He leans back and spreads his legs a bit. I can see the bulge in his pants. He wants me as bad as I want him. I hesitate. I want this, but I don't want him to think this is something I do all the time. I start playing with the lace on my dress, trying to come up with the right words.

"This isn't normal for me; I want you to know that. I don't jump from guy to guy."

"The thought never crossed my mind. All I'm thinking is that we are two adults, neither one of us is currently seeing anyone, and we're clearly attracted to one another. I've been watching you squirm in your seat for the past few minutes, and I'm feeling it, too." He motions toward the bulge in his pants. "Tell me you don't want this, that you don't want *me,* and we won't do anything. It won't change how I feel toward you, Kaylan."

I don't think I have ever gotten out of my seat so fast. I pull up my dress and climb into his lap, my knees resting on either side of his hips. I grab his face with my hands and pull it to mine, our lips connecting. The kiss is hot and needy, and I am panting and moaning immediately. He takes control and slides his tongue along the seam of my lips. I open willingly for him as our tongues dance. His hands grab my ass and I moan into him, rocking my hips back and forth.

As he pulls away, I watch him. His pupils are huge, his lips are kiss-swollen red, and his cheeks are flushed. Seeing him in this state makes me whimper, and he chuckles darkly. "Maybe we should take this inside? We don't need to give the neighbors a show." He motions towards the house behind me.

I smile and lift my hips off his, kneeling above him, and reach my hand down between us, reaching for his zipper. He moans as my hand brushes over him, and he lets his head fall back. I pull him free, making sure my dress still covers the two of us, and give him a few gentle strokes. "Where's the fun in that? Besides, it's almost completely dark and my dress will hide us." I lean in so I'm whispering in his ear. "Please, Jack, if I move from your lap I might lose my nerve. Please fuck me here."

An animalistic noise escapes from his throat. He pulls my

panties to the side, grips my hips tightly, and pulls me down on top of him until he bottoms out. I bury my face in the side of his neck and begin peppering him with kisses. His thrusts are hard and fast, and he's gripping my hips so tight I know I will have bruises in the morning. I grind my hips down on him, his jeans rubbing against my clit, creating enough friction I begin to spiral.

"Jack, I'm getting close," I pant.

"I'm there with you. Come for me, Kaylan. Let me feel you," he groans and bites my shoulder. It's all I need, my orgasm taking over. I bury my face in his shoulder again to keep my noises down so as not to alarm the neighbors. I feel it as soon as he lets go, his warmth flooding through me and his thrusts slowing until he finally stops. The two of us are breathing heavy and still connected. I lift my head and place my forehead on his, and we sit still, breathing each other in. His eyes pop open wide with panic.

"Shit, I didn't pull out. We didn't use protection."

"I have an implant. It's fine."

"That was *not* how I expected our first time. That was too quick. I've been thinking about you for the past few weeks, what it would be like to feel you. I was too excited. I'm gonna make it up to you." He places his lips on mine and tangles his fingers through my hair, pulling me as close to him as I can get. His cock is still in me and I feel him twitch, knowing if we keep this up he is going to get hard again. I pull back and smile at him.

"Maybe we should clean up and then we can try this again later if you want?" I lift my hips, and we both groan as he slips out.

He lifts his eyebrows. "So, by later, do you mean tonight or a different night?" He tucks himself back into his pants as I fix my soaked panties, thinking it might be better to take them off. I stand anyway and allow him to stand up and wrap his arm around my waist. "If you mean tonight, I am more than happy to have a house guest for the evening, but there is no pressure. I know we're getting up early to bake at the restaurant, and if you want your sleep, I am happy to take you home."

I play with my dress again and look down at the ground. "I'd like to stay the night if that's all right with you?" I ask, unsure of my own decision. I peek up at him through my lashes and see a smile spread across his face. Cradling my face in his large hands, he plants a light kiss on my lips.

"That's more than okay with me. What time do you have to get up in the morning?"

"I need to start baking by four or so. Not sure how long it takes to get to the restaurant from here though."

He looks at his watch and then back at me. "How much sleep are you planning on getting?" He cocks an eyebrow in question.

"That all depends on what you have in mind for the evening?" I smirk, knowing where he's going with this.

His eyes darken, and I notice a small twitch in his pants. "I have a lot of things in mind, but I know you are going to have a full day of baking, too, and I want you to get some sleep if that's what you want."

"How about we have dessert and see where the night takes us? Does that sound good?"

He smiles, clearly liking my answer. "I think that's perfect. I can't wait to try these special brownies anyway. What did you put in them to make them so special?

"You'll just have to taste them to find out, won't you?"

CHAPTER TEN

$\mathcal{T}$he next morning, I wake up with Jack pressed against my back and his arm draped around my waist. The clock on the dresser reads two thirty-eight, which means I still have a little bit of time before I have to get up. I lay my hand on top of his, and I hear him shift and groan quietly.

"What time is it?" he mutters, burrowing his head in my hair and planting kisses along my neck.

I tilt my head to the side, giving him more access. "It's almost two forty. We still have a little more time to sleep." I stifle a yawn as I finish. When he rocks his hips forward, I feel his erection pressing against me and my body hums awake.

"We could, or we could try to go for round two. I promised to make it up to you, and since you basically passed out on me after dessert last night, I would really like the chance to."

He kisses my shoulder and turns me so I'm on my back. He presses half his body weight into me and kisses my lips, his tongue sliding into my willing mouth. I sigh and run my fingers down the sides of his body, feeling the muscles flex under my touch.

"I think I like that idea the best," I reply, stopping my hands on the waistband of his shorts, running my fingers along his taut stomach and through the small amount of hair around his navel. He takes a deep breath in and exhales it slowly, his breathing ragged. He grips my right hand in his and drags it under the waistband so I can wrap my fingers around his shaft. I slide my hand up and down, feeling it twitch under my fingers. He thrusts his hips back and forth to gain more friction.

He hooks his thumbs in the waistband of my panties. "I want to taste you, Kaylan."

I remove my hand from him, give a slight nod of my head, and lift my hips, allowing him to pull them down my legs. I'm lying there bare from the waist down, my chest covered with one of his t-shirts. He kisses the inside of my thigh, making a trail to my core, his scruff tickling my sensitive skin. He flicks his tongue over my clit, and I arch my back off the bed, digging my fingers into his hair, scratching his scalp. He tests the waters and gives a few gentle licks, watching my body react after each one.

He drapes his arm over my waist to hold me in place as he dives in, lapping his tongue up and down my folds. He inserts two fingers into me, and it's exactly what my body needs. I'm a panting mess. "Please, Jack." I pull him closer, and he picks up the pace, eating me out like he is starving, trying to push me over the edge. He curls his fingers over my g-spot, and I feel as if I'm going to pass out. The flick of his tongue, the curl of his fingers—it's all too much. Finally, he curls his fingers inside of me, adding more pressure to my g-spot, and I let go, soaking his face. He continues licking at me as he works me through my high and then pulls away with a huge smile on his lips.

"That was so hot. I'm going to have to remember that for future." He wipes his mouth and crawls on top of me, lowering his lips to mine so I can taste myself on him. I wrap my legs around his waist and buck my hips up, needing to feel him inside me again. Whimpering, I realize his shorts are still on, and I try to push them down with my heels. He chuckles against my lips and sits up to pull them down his legs and off. "Take your shirt off," he commands and I pull it over my head, the both of us now naked. He smiles as his eyes roam down over my body, and I feel my breathing hitch. "You're so beautiful, Kaylan."

He grabs himself and lines himself up with my entrance. Lifting my left leg over his waist, he slowly presses in, both of us moaning at the feel of one another. He holds still, allowing me to adjust to him, and I rock my hips, needing to feel him move. He moves, thrusting a little faster and harder. I grip the sheets in my hands and close my eyes, focusing on the feel of him moving inside me.

"You feel amazing, Kay. You fit me so well," he groans, picking up the pace. I rub my clit, already feeling myself clenching around him. He pulls my other leg over his shoulder, allowing for a deeper thrust, and begins working his hips faster, chasing his release. "I can't hold off, babe. Are you there?" he asks, his hips stuttering.

"Come for me, Jack. Let me feel you."

His thrusts change from smooth to jerky as he lets go, his release setting mine off. The two of us are a moaning sweaty mess as we come down together. We stay still, and I clench around him one more time, eliciting a groan from him as I pull my leg off his shoulder.

"Can I take a shower? Also, since I wasn't planning on spending the night, I need clothes to bake in. Can we run by my place to get some items?"

"Sure, let's take a quick shower and I'll take you home so we can gather whatever items you need for today." He gives me a quick kiss on the lips and helps me sit up. "That was amazing. I could get used to waking up like that." He smiles.

"Yeah, I could, too."

WE GET BACK to my place so I can change out of the dress and get all the baking items into his car to get started for the day. "Kaylan, can I entice you to get breakfast with me?"

"Well, since I knew I was going to be baking at the restaurant instead of the bakery, I premade a lot of stuff last night, which means I have a bit more time today than normal. Breakfast sounds nice." I agree and his stomach rumbles.

"Sorry," he mumbles as he pats his flat stomach. "I normally don't get my workout in until later in the morning so I'm starving." He smiles sheepishly. "Do you want to go to the diner?"

"One day, I will get a home cooked meal from *you*, mister." I laugh. "But, yes, the diner sounds good to me. Can I get out of this dress before we do that then? I also don't have on any," I pause and feel the heat rise to my cheeks, "panties, and I would rather change into something more comfortable so it doesn't look like the walk of shame."

He takes my hand in his and pulls it up to his lips, brushing a gentle kiss on the back of my knuckles. "Knowing you have on nothing under that dress, babe, is doing all sorts of things to me. It's probably best if you get some on."

We go up to my apartment, and I change quickly into a blue fitted t-shirt and a pair of workout capris and walk back into the living room where Jack is waiting patiently. He smiles and reaches out for me, pulling me toward him, and plants a heated kiss on my lips. I'm ravenous and want more, but he breaks away.

"What was that for?" I ask.

"Even in workout clothes, you're beautiful and I can't get enough of you. I know we're supposed to be taking things slow..." He pauses, appraising my response when my eyes shoot up. He holds his hands up in defense. "And we are. I won't push anything. I just want you to hear it often and believe me when I say it."

"Thank you, Jack," I murmur quietly. "I'm ready to go. Do you want to walk or drive over?"

"Let's drive, it will save some time. It should be a pretty quick meal. I don't imagine many people are up this early for breakfast." He takes my hand and we walk back down to his car. He opens the door, and once I am seated, closes it behind me. I watch him get into the car, and I keep staring at him. He smiles over at me and asks, "What?"

"You're just a really nice guy. What's wrong with you? What's your fault? You seem too perfect."

His smile falters before he screws his features back and teases, "Nah, I'm just perfect. You'll see."

He pulls into the diner and we get out of the car. He places his hand gently on my lower back and leads me to the front door, pulling it open and ushering me inside. Looking around, there are only five or six other people besides the wait staff and cooks. It really is dead.

"Jack, I didn't expect to see you back so soon. Oh, Kaylan, nice to see you again too dear." Steph smirks as she picks up two menus and leads us towards a table.

"Morning, Steph, nice to see you again as well. You're here early."

"It's my favorite shift. You two are up early, too." She places the menus down in front of us and walks away, leaving us to look over them.

"You know she is going to call me later and want all the details, right? Either that, or she's calling my mother, and *she* will call me to make a big deal out of it." He laughs and winks at me.

"Oh yeah? So, what are you going to tell her exactly?"

He lowers his voice and leans forward so the conversation is private. "I'm going to tell her it's none of her damn business and that I am allowed a few secrets." He smiles, and I return the gesture.

"Well, that's good. I never liked when men felt they had to kiss and tell."

We order and carry on a quiet conversation as each of us drink our coffee. He gets up to use the restroom, and I pull out my phone and check some emails. I see a response from Dan agreeing on the new pricing plan, stating it could help a bit, but we still have to look into alternatives to get more cash flow. I type a quick response of thanks and put my phone away, not wanting to look at work emails yet.

"Hot date later?" Jack asks, sliding back into the booth.

"I don't know, are you offering?" I smirk.

"That all depends. Would you say yes?"

I shrug my shoulders as our plates of food are put down in front of us. We both thank the waitress and dig into it. I ordered a vegetable omelet with a side of bacon and toast, and he got a meat-lovers one with the same. The food is delicious and hits the spot, both of us eating quickly so we can get to the restaurant to bake.

"Have you ever baked before?" I ask as we exit the restaurant and head toward his car to get the supplies.

"When I was little with my mom. We used to bake sugar cookies a lot."

"That's sweet. Do you see her often?" When he doesn't answer right away, I turn to look at him. His jaw is tight and his face rigid as stone.

"No." He opens the car door and closes it behind me a little harder than he means to. When he gets into his side, he says, "Sorry. It's not something I want to talk about right now. I'm good at following instructions, so if you tell me what to do, I can do that."

WE PACK the car quickly and make it to the restaurant at just after four. Carrying all the items into the kitchen, my jaw goes slack. Everything is so nice and shiny and *huge*; it is apparent Oliver takes a lot of pride in his kitchen.

"Are you sure Oliver is okay with this? I don't want to mess up his kitchen. It's so clean and shiny."

"He won't even know we were here, and if so, I'll take the rap for it." He drops the items in his arms on the counter and heads back to the car to get more stuff. I turn on the oven to begin preheating it and go to the sink to wash my hands. I'm humming to myself when Jack slides his arms around me and rests his chin on my shoulder. He places his hands under the water and begins washing his as well, his breathing tickling my ear.

"You know, you keep this up and the kitchen is going to end up a whole lot dirtier, and I'm pretty sure that would be several health code violations," I tease, leaning back against him.

His voice is deep and husky. "I won't tell if you won't." He grazes my ear with his teeth and nibbles on it gently before backing away. I stand there, trying to get my heart rate to return to normal before I finally turn to look at him.

"You're trouble, aren't you?"

He feigns shock and puts a hand to his chest. "Never. It's not *my* fault you were standing there looking beautiful. It's also not *my* fault I had to wash my hands if I'm going to help you, and you were standing there."

"Okay, buddy, whatever you say." I pull the apron over my head and throw one in his direction. He follows my lead and ties it around his slim waist before rubbing his hands together excitedly.

"So, what am I helping you with first?"

I pick up a bowl filled with batter and place it in front of him. "I need you to make cake balls. You have to make sure they are about the same size. I sucked at this when I first started, so I brought over the scoop, too, in case you need it." When I hand him the scoop, he looks at it and places it on the counter, ignoring it as he goes to work. His cake balls are almost perfect, and I school my features to not let him see how impressed I am.

I begin making the batter for the éclairs. The two of us work well together. He finishes what I ask him to do just as I am starting to fill the pastry bag with the mixture. After washing his hands, he comes back and stands behind me, placing his hands on my hips.

"Care to teach me?" he asks, peppering my neck with kisses.

Turning my head to the side, I look at him before his lips meet mine. I place the pastry bag on the table so I can turn my body toward his. I wrap my arms around his neck and deepen the kiss, his tongue gliding with mine effortlessly. Moaning, I lean into his touch, his hands tangling in my hair as he pulls me closer. Everything seems to come to a standstill; time doesn't seem to matter when we are together. Reluctantly, I pull away and look him in the eyes. Jack does something to me. He makes me feel as if I'm enough just by being me. I'm falling for him, and I'm falling fast.

"Penny for your thoughts?" he asks.

I look down, avoiding his beautiful, gleaming eyes, and play with the side of my apron. "I don't know. Let's just get back to work." I pick up the pastry bag and hand it to him. "Come on, I'll show you how to make them and then we can melt the chocolate for the cake balls."

He holds the tipped end in his left hand and the twisted top in his right. "Now, you want to hold the bag at about a forty-five-degree angle and apply even pressure through the entire process. You want to make the éclair about four inches long, and then you want to pull the bag away. Think you can handle it?" I ask, looking up at him.

"I wish you would tell me what you are really thinking, Kaylan. I can see there is something else you want to say."

He follows my instructions, not pressing the subject, and makes a perfect éclair first time out.

"My aunt taught you a lot more than you're letting on, Jack. Just how much did you help her with? You said odds and ends..." I trail off.

"I liked being in the kitchen, and she taught me a few tricks. Never her recipes though. Just how to help create the master-pieces," he says sheepishly.

I hum my response and turn away to melt chocolate for the cake balls. "Once you finish with those, they need to go in the oven for ten minutes, and then we need to dip these and get the whoopie pies made."

We work in silence for another minute before he finally speaks again. "Kaylan? Did I do something wrong?"

I turn and look at him, his face scrunched in concern. I let out a small sigh. "No, I'm just being stupid. Sorry. We were having a nice morning, and I ruined it because I think too much. Can we just forget it for now?"

"I wish you'd tell me what you were thinking, what I did to change your demeanor."

I sigh again and rub my forehead, turning the heat down so the chocolate won't burn. "Kevin and I just broke up yesterday, and *we* have already had sex—twice." I give him a sly smile. "It really is happening fast, and I'm scared you're just a rebound. You're too nice to be a rebound." He smiles and my heart skips a beat. *I just told him I'm scared, and he's looking back at me like I'm the most amazing thing in the entire world. I am so screwed.*

"Kaylan?" He takes a step closer and grabs my hands. "I told you we would move slowly. Yes, last night was a lot all at once, but we can back off. We can slow it down. You let me know what you need and I'll do it." He gives my hands a gentle squeeze and drops them in favor of the pastry bag.

We finish baking everything and clean up the kitchen, making sure to leave it as spotless as before. Carefully, we pack up the car with the baked goods and take them over to the shop. We arrive at the same time as Denise, and she helps us get everything inside and into the display cases.

"Hey, Denise, can you and Jack finish setting everything up? I need to update a few things in the office."

She agrees and I leave the two of them to their quiet conversation as they load the display cases. *I hope she does not do or say anything to embarrass me.* I open the pricing program and update everything to the agreed-upon prices that I sent to Dan. Jessica walks in and drops her stuff off, saying good morning in the process.

"Hey, Jessica, I want to give you a heads up. The prices of everything have gone up a bit, so I don't want you to be alarmed when you see it on the register."

"Sheryl never changed the prices. Why are you?" she asks, annoyed.

I should not have to explain myself to her. "I think it will be better for the bakery. The cost of supplies has gone up over the years, and I'm sure Sheryl didn't factor that in." I smile nicely at her and watch her roll her eyes and walk toward the front of the store. *I have no idea what I did to piss her off, but I wish she would just tell me!* She passes Jack and gives him a small wave as he makes his way back to the office.

"Hey, I'm going to head out now."

"Okay. Thank you again for all your help and for allowing me to use the kitchen at the restaurant. I truly appreciate it."

"Not a problem. What time is the guy coming today?"

"He said between nine and ten this morning, so within a few

hours. Hopefully, he can fix it. I can't deal with having to get a new oven, too." I stand on tip-toes and give him a gentle kiss on the cheek. "Thanks for everything. I'll see you later."

He grabs me and pulls me in for a hug, burying his head in my hair, inhaling deeply. Finally, he lets go and places a soft kiss on my cheek. "See you later." He turns and walks out of the kitchen, leaving me alone. I smile and place my hand on my cheek as Denise walks in.

"You have a lot of explaining to do, missy," she says, hands planted firmly on her hips.

CHAPTER ELEVEN

ednesday evening after I close the shop for the night, I decide to get a few items from my apartment in the city. Since I know Kevin isn't going to be there, I figure it's best to do it now. I hop on the freeway a little after five-thirty and, thankfully, traffic isn't too bad. I make it home in about an hour and walk inside the apartment. Looking around, it seems as if an explosion has gone off. There are dishes in the sink, clothes on the back of chairs, and a few empty beer cans on the kitchen counter.

What the hell happened here? Kevin is always so put together, and he keeps things so organized. He must be a lot more stressed than I thought. The thought tugs at my heart a bit, and at that moment, I feel horrible for sleeping with Jack. *We are taking time apart, a break.* It's the mantra I keep repeating over and over. I begin picking up the apartment and tidying it up a bit. Dishes are put in the dishwasher, suit jackets get hung up in the closet, and panties are dropped in the dirty clothes hamper. *Wait. Panties? I haven't been home in weeks.*

I pick the offensive piece of fabric up with my finger and look at it. These are *not* mine. I don't wear hot pink sparkly panties. I feel the anger begin to rise. *We are taking time apart, a break.* I no longer feel horrible for sleeping with Jack; in fact, I feel relieved. I stop cleaning and opt to pack up all the items I can that belong to me, sans the furniture.

After several trips to my car, I have ninety percent of my personal items packed up. I walk back into the apartment and scribble a note of a scrap piece of paper, stick it on top of the panties, and leave both on the dining room table. I'm hurt, and angry, and in desperate need of a drink. I know I will be receiving a call in a few days when Kevin gets back, and I'm not looking forward to *that* conversation. I open my texts and begin a new one to my girlfriend, Katie.

Me: *Hey, are you up for drinks? I'm in the city right now and would love to catch up.*

Katie: *Would love to! Can you meet in 30 mins at Rock Bottom?*

Me: *Yep, see you then.*

Thank God for Katie!

WORK IS BECOMING MORE and more of a nightmare. I find myself sneaking off to the bakery more often just to get away from the clients for a few minutes. The new prices have been in effect for the past week, and business doesn't seem to be any worse, so I'm breathing easy for that. I do need to figure out what to do in order to get more business drummed up, and I decide it's time to let Denise and Jessica in on everything.

I walk into the bakery and notice Jessica helping a customer who is chewing her ear off.

"I have been coming here for years, and the price of cream puffs has always been the same. Why is it suddenly fifty cents higher? This is ridiculous. The previous owner would never have allowed this to happen," the elderly woman rants.

Jessica looks at up me, flustered. There is a line behind the woman, and I can tell other customers are getting frustrated listening to her rant and rave.

"Excuse me, ma'am. My name's Kaylan Santine, and I'm the current owner of *Little Sweet Shoppe*. I would like to hear your concerns. Would you please join me at the table?" I ask, motioning toward an empty table furthest away from the case. She huffs and snatches her cream puff from Jessica before storming over to the table. I sit down opposite her and put a smile on my face. *Kill them with kindness.* "What's your name, ma'am?"

"My name is Eleanor, and you are too young to be running this establishment."

I keep my smile in place, not wanting to show weakness. "Hello, Eleanor, I'm Sheryl Albert's niece. I hear you have a few complaints. I'd like the chance to talk to you and, hopefully, we can resolve some of the issues." I begin talking to this woman as if she was one of my clients, trying to put her at ease.

"Yes, well for starters, I've never seen you around here. Your aunt was out here greeting the customers all the time. She treated each of us like family. Also, the price of these has gone up. Why? Your aunt hadn't raised prices in over five years. You come in, and within a month, prices are going through the roof. Are you just trying to steal our money?" She is glaring at me, but she takes a deep breath and takes a bite of her cream puff. "You're lucky the baking tastes as good as hers; otherwise, I would be taking my business elsewhere."

"Eleanor, I'm sorry you feel this way. The first item you

brought up, me not being here? I am usually in the back or working at my other job, so I can't be out here as often as I should. You are correct though. My aunt was always around, and I will make a point to be here more often going forward." I watch as she takes another bite of her treat and nods her head in approval. "As far as the prices go, I had to raise them because the cost of supplies has gone up. We are actually making less for each item we sell now than we did five years ago. I'm doing what has to be done to keep the business afloat and still pay my employees."

"You say you're working another job right now. How can you dedicate the time to this place if the other job is eating up your time?"

This woman isn't going to hold anything back. "Yes, I am currently working two jobs. It was a complete shock when my aunt left me the store. I assumed she would be leaving it to my uncle. I have a life in the city, and I'm not sure if this is what I want to do long term. I am enjoying this right now, and I'm learning a lot, but I can't uproot my life entirely until I know for sure this is what I want to do. For the time being, I am working both jobs, and if the opportunity arises to switch careers, and I want to make that leap, then I will."

"You could make that choice if you wanted to right now. You're just too scared. That's why the shop isn't doing as well. People can smell the fear." She finishes her food and stands up. I stand with her and give her the sweetest smile I can muster. "If you want to keep this place running, you need to focus on it more." With that final word of advice, she walks out of the store.

I look around and notice a few customers looking at me, without doubt listening to the exchange between us. *Is she right? Do people know I'm afraid?* I smile at Jessica, and she mouths 'thank you' to me. I gather the woman's plate and clean up the table before I help her behind the counter for a few minutes. When the last of the customers files out, I turn to her.

"How often have you been hearing that same complaint?"

"What, the complaint about *you* not being here, or the prices?" she asks, crossing her arms over her chest.

I mirror her stance. "Both."

"Basically, since you started and since you updated the prices," she responds matter-of-factly.

"Jessica, can we sit and talk for a minute?" I ask, gesturing toward the same table. She shrugs and walks over, pulling the seat out and plopping down. I take a seat and place my hands on the table, trying to keep myself as open as possible. "Jess, the bakery isn't doing well. I've had to try to make a few adjustments to keep us on target. That includes increasing the prices. I ran the numbers by Dan, my financial guy, and he agreed this would be a good start. I'm just trying to keep you and Denise working and the business open."

"Are you paying yourself, too? If so, you could always stop that."

I shake my head. "No, I am relying on my other job. I'm not making anything off this place. Honestly, I am here because my uncle asked me to and because I know how much this place meant to my aunt. If you have any suggestions to keep the bakery running, I'm all ears."

Her mood changes as soon as I ask for her advice. "Does Denise know?"

"I have a feeling she does, but I haven't told her yet. Maybe now is the time to." I take a deep breath. "Denise, can you come out here?" I call back to her. I hear a few pans being put down before I see her walk through the swinging door.

"What's going on, hun?" she asks as she takes a seat. "Looks like we're having a pow-wow out here."

"Jessica and I were talking about why some things have changed around here, and I want to make sure you are in the loop as well. I raised the prices a week ago for everything in the bakery. I just dealt with a customer who was irritated that the prices had gone up, and I want to explain why. Jess told me she has been dealing with it all week, too. The shop hasn't been doing as well since Aunt Sheryl passed away. This price increase was the fastest solution to generate more revenue for us. I'm afraid if we don't start selling more soon, I am going to have to let someone go or close up shop. If either of you has suggestions, I'd love to hear them. I need both of you in order to keep this place running." I look at each of them, neither one of them wanting to look me in the eyes.

"How long?" Jessica asks.

"A few months, if things don't turn around."

"Sheryl used to have people come here from time to time wanting to have her sell at their stores. Maybe that is a route you can explore?" Denise asks as she places her hand on mine, a small smile tugging at her lips. "We will find a way. Sheryl always did.

"That's a good idea, Denise. Do you happen to know who used to come by to ask?"

Her smile fades. "No, I don't. She might have some business cards lying around somewhere though."

"Thanks, I'll check through the office."

The bell above the front door jingles and Jack walks in, a big smile on his face until he sees the three of us sitting there looking glum. "Hey, everyone," he says, looking between the three of us.

"Hey, Jack. Here for your éclair?" I ask, giving him a small smile.

He nods his head and tilts it to the side, examining us. "Is everything okay?"

"Yep, we're fine." I stand, and Jessica and Denise do the same. *Meeting adjourned.* Denise heads back into the kitchen, and Jessica walks behind the counter to get his treat. She puts it on a plate, and he hands her money as he takes the plate from her. He throws the leftover change in the tip jar and it makes me smile.

He murmurs his thanks, walking over to the table, motioning for me to take a seat.

"Are you sure everything's all right? The conversation you seemed to be having seemed a bit tense. Can I help with anything?"

I chuckle and shake my head. "It's fine. Thanks though, I appreciate your help." The last thing I want to do is tell him how things aren't looking much better. I don't need him concerned about this. I watch as he takes a bite and holds it out to me, asking if I want one. I shake my head. I need to start working out again. My clothes are starting to become a little snug.

"It's good. Are you sure?" he asks, trying to entice me.

"I'm good. My clothes are fitting a little tighter. I've been eating too much sugar as it is."

He smirks and leans in closer to whisper, "Maybe we need to work out together a bit more? I'll give you a good workout."

My face turns ten shades of red, and I stammer, "T-that's not what I meant. I meant going for a run or something." I place my cold hands over my cheeks to try and cool them off.

"I'll run with you. When do you want to go?" He finishes his éclair and wipes his mouth and hands with the napkin.

"Are you working later today?"

"I don't have to be."

"Jack, I don't want to get you in trouble. I feel like I'm taking a lot of your time. If you have to go into the restaurant, please go. We can go tomorrow morning after I finish baking. It's not a problem." Our conversation is interrupted by my phone. I looked at the caller ID and see it is Kevin. I feel my stomach jump into my throat and think I might be sick. I look at Jack, my eyes wide, and show him who is calling before answering.

"Hello?" I stand and walk outside to have a semi-private conversation.

"Kaylan, I'm back from my trip and I wanted to talk." His tone is snippy.

"Well, I can't at the moment. I'm a bit busy."

"We need to talk about the note you left me and why you basically moved out."

I feel my throat constrict and the tears burning my eyes. "No, we don't. We're on a break. You can fuck whoever you want."

"Fuck, Kaylan," he practically yells. "We are going to talk about this. I'm coming down this weekend. We are not leaving things like this."

I look through the window at Jack, who is watching me avidly, concern etched on his face. I sigh heavily. "Kev, I don't want you down here. We will talk this weekend or something and figure out how to sort through the rest of our stuff, but *don't* come down."

He growls through the phone and hangs up, not saying another word. I pull the phone away from my ear and turn my back to the window. I don't want Jack to see me so upset. I hear the door open behind me and then feel his strong arms wrap around my waist, his chin resting on my shoulder. "I'm here if you want to talk."

I shake my head and pat his arm before breaking away from his embrace. "I need to get back to work. I'm fine. Thank you though." I refuse to face him and try to go up the steps to my apartment. He grabs my arm and I turn to look at him.

"Don't shut me out, Kaylan. Please don't. I've had people shut me out when I needed support, and I want you to know I won't do that to you. Whatever you need, I'm here."

I nod my head and gently pull my arm from his grasp. "Thanks, Jack. We'll talk later. I'll explain everything to you then."

I pull my laptop into my lap and log into my bank account. I look at the joint account I have with Kevin and the amount of money in it. Some of the money in that account is mine, and I keep thinking about how that would help the shop so much. I shake the idea from my head and begin looking up shops in the area that might be interested in carrying our treats.

The day wears on, and the emails from my other job are piling up, but I'm too consumed with trying to locate someone who might want to start carrying our stuff. I run down to the bakery several times, looking for any leads I can find, but come up short. Looks like Aunt Sheryl didn't want to keep any of that info handy.

I'm making my last call of the day when the downstairs buzzer goes off. I walk over to the buzzer and answer, "Hello?"

"Kaylan, it's me. Can I come up?" Jack asks. I respond by hitting the buzzer, allowing him access to my apartment. Within seconds, he is knocking on the door; he must have sprinted up them. I open it and lean against the side of the door, watching him. "Hey, I've been worried. You haven't returned any of my texts today. Are you all right?"

"Sorry, I've had a lot on my mind and I've been pretty busy. I didn't even notice you had texted me." It's a lie; I saw the texts as they came in, and I chose to ignore them. I wasn't ready to talk to him yet, and I knew he would want to know what happened between me and Kevin. He pulls me into a hug, and I allow him to, but I don't wrap my arms around him.

"Kay, talk to me. What's wrong? What did Kevin say on the phone today?" He pulls back and studies my face. I stare at him, not wanting to talk. "Please, Kaylan, you told me we would talk later. I don't want to pressure you either, but I want you to know I'm here. It would mean a lot to me if you open up and tell me." His tone is all but pleading.

I sigh heavily and shake my head as if I were shaking away cobwebs. "Thanks, Jack. That means a lot to me. I've just been swamped today with work and things for the bakery. I don't want to talk about Kevin right now. I promise, when I'm ready, you are the first person I will come to, all right?"

He nods his head, content with the answer. "I ordered food. I figure you probably haven't eaten a whole lot today. I wanted to make sure you got food in your system, and then since we are running tomorrow morning, I wanted to just finalize the time. Would nine be okay for you? I know you have to bake first."

"Sure, nine sounds great. Thank you, Jack, for everything. I have one more favor to ask if you're willing. No pressure."

He smiles. "Anything for you, sugar."

"Would you stay here with me tonight? I really don't want to go to bed alone, and I could use someone to cuddle up with—"

He cuts me off by placing his finger over my lips. "I'll stay as long as you need me to." He smiles and I melt into him, hugging him around his slim waist and inhaling the scent that is all him.

"Thank you," I murmur into his chest as I feel a tear slide down my cheek.

CHAPTER TWELVE

I wake early the next morning to Jack wrapped around me. I remember falling asleep on the couch after eating a little something, and he must have carried me to bed. I don't even remember getting into pajamas, but here I am in a t-shirt and panties. I sit up enough to look at the clock. It's still early and I have a bit more time to sleep. Snuggling back down, I try to get comfortable and place my arm over Jack's.

"If you keep moving like that, you're going to make me want you more than I already do," he mumbles.

"Oh yeah?" I wiggle my butt against his crotch and feel his hard length pressing into me. He reaches his hand down and begins rubbing me through my panties, rocking his hips into me so I can feel him more. I toss my right leg over his hip, allowing him easier access to my core. A contented sigh escapes my lips as he slips his fingers under the waistband of my panties and begins drawing small circles on my clit.

"So wet already. Were you having nice dreams of me?" He chuckles as he kisses my neck and collarbone, his other hand kneading my breast roughly.

"Please, Jack," I whimper. "I need more than this." He pulls his hand away from me, pulls his boxers down around his ass, and pulls my panties to the side. He rubs his cock through my folds, slicking it up with my wetness before he gently presses in. Placing his hand on my lower stomach, he holds me in place as he rocks back and forth, his cock stretching me nicely.

"You feel so good, Kaylan. I want to be here all the time," he groans, picking up the pace. I reach my hand down and stroke my clit. My body feels as if it's on fire. Our breathing is heavy, and our moans fill the small bedroom. We work in tandem to bring each other to release. "Kaylan, tell me you're close. I can feel you squeezing me, and I can't hold out much longer."

"Oh fuck, harder, Jack. I'm so close," I pant, every muscle in my body clenching as I work toward my release. He grips my hip a little tighter and snakes his fingers down over mine, adding more pressure to my clit. I hit my orgasm hard, clenching around him, moaning loudly as I feel him pump a few more times and finally release into me. After a few more thrusts to finish riding his high, he stops. Kissing me on the shoulder, he pulls out and gets out of bed.

"I'll get a wet towel to clean us up."

"No, let's just take a quick shower. I'll sleep better if we do that." I throw the covers back and take off my shirt, standing in front of him naked. He does the same, stripping out of his boxers. My eyes roam over his naked form, and I watch his muscles flex under my attentive gaze. I look down at my own body and begin trying to cover myself.

"Don't you dare." He strides over and stands in front of me, pulling my hands away from my body. "I want to be able to see you. You're perfect, and I don't want you to feel any different."

"I've put on a little weight though," I say, looking toward the ground.

"I don't think you have. You look amazing. Your body is

perfect, just like the rest of you. Please don't cover yourself from me. If you are not happy with your body then change it. I'll help any way I can." He smiles and dips his finger under my chin so I can look up into his eyes. I wrap my arms around his body and pull him close to me for a tight hug. His arms wrap around my waist, and he kisses the top of my head. "Come on, let's get cleaned up and back in bed."

I pile my hair up on top of my head and let the hot water cascade down my body. He picks up the washcloth and begins washing my back for me, his hands moving gently over my skin.

"He fucked someone, and I've basically moved out of our apartment," I blurt out. "I don't know how long he's been doing it. I don't want to know, either. I found her panties when I went to the apartment this week, and I left a nasty message. When he called me yesterday, he said he wanted to come down to explain, but, honestly, I don't want to see him right now." I feel his hands still and I turn to look at him, trying to read his expression.

"What did the note say?"

"I hope you get syphilis and your dick falls off."

He laughs so hard I fear he is going to fall over in the shower. "Oh my God, that's amazing! You seriously wrote that in the note?" He grabs his stomach and doubles over laughing as I shake my head, my own laughter starting. "Well, shit, I know not to mess with you now." He takes a minute to reign in his laughter and says, "Seriously, though, I'm sorry that's how you had to find out about it. But it is bad to say I'm happy?"

I furrow my brows and my jaw goes slack as I stare at him in disbelief. "Why does that make you happy? I just found out I was being cheated on."

"I'm happy because that means that I can be more for you. I really like you, Kaylan, and I'll do whatever I can to keep you." He leans down and kisses me gently on the lips, pulling back seconds later. "I want you to know how much I like you, that I will do almost anything for you."

THE ALARM STARTLES ME AWAKE, and I turn quickly to shut off the annoying buzz. Groaning, I get out of bed to freshen up, leaving Jack looking comfortable. After a few minutes, I return and he is getting into his clothes.

"What are you doing? You can stay in bed while I go bake. I trust you."

"Oh. I figured since you were leaving, I should, too," he replies as he runs his fingers through his luscious chestnut locks. I watch his hand and begin picturing myself tugging his hair as eats me out. Wetness pools between my legs. He is watching me intently before smiling. "You're having naughty thoughts right now, aren't you?"

I blush. "I have no idea *what* you're talking about." I pull my bottom lip between my teeth and smile sweetly.

He leans in so his face is inches from mine. "Were you thinking about me shoving my cock deep inside your wet pussy and fucking you hard? Or maybe you were thinking about me between your soft thighs, my tongue on you?" His lust-filled eyes lock with mine, and I let out a tiny needy whimper. He smirks. "It's my tongue, isn't it?"

I nod my head. "I had a very vivid image of me tugging your hair as you're eating me out." I hear a small hiss escape his lips and he closes his eyes, clearly imagining it as well. "It will have to wait until later though. I'm running a bit behind now and need to get downstairs."

"Tell you what, your reward for working out will be that. Anytime you finish a workout, I will congratulate you with an orgasm. Keep you on track."

"I think that is more for you than for me, but I'll take it." I laugh. I give him a quick kiss on the lips and leave him in the bedroom to start my morning. I am so glad it is already Saturday and the bakery will be closed tomorrow. I need a day to catch up on everything, and I'll need time alone to talk to Kevin. I just hope he doesn't come down like I requested; he's the last person I want to see.

THE MORNING FLIES BY; Jack strolls down to the shop around eight toting a few coffees and some muffins for us.

"Good Morning Jack." Denise opens the front door, allowing him to enter. "What brings you in so early? You know we aren't open until nine, and you probably shouldn't have an éclair this early anyway," Denise teases.

"I came in to see your beautiful face. Plus, I figure you could use food and coffee. I thought it might win me a few brownie points." He looks at me and winks, a smile gracing his face.

"You didn't come to see my old haggard face, son. I know who you're really here to see. You two go grab a table and I'll be out in a few minutes." She shoos us out of the kitchen, and he pulls the chair out for me. I sit and he takes the seat across from me. He hands me a coffee, and I thank him as I take a sip, the flavors melting on my tongue.

"This is great. Where's it from?" I ask, digging into the muffin as well.

"There's a small café close to my house that makes the best coffee, so I wanted to get you some. I ran home to get workout clothes and thought you would appreciate the extra caffeine. I have a tough workout planned for you."

"Hopefully, my reward will be well deserved then." I laugh

and break off another piece of the blueberry muffin, popping it in my mouth.

"Hmm, your reward. I can't wait to taste that. I bet it will be like heaven on my tongue." He licks his lips and smiles darkly.

"What will be? Your éclair?" Denise asks, walking out to join us.

He doesn't miss a beat. "Yep, exactly. They always taste so good. I don't know how you ladies do it; it's a gift for sure."

"Well, maybe you'd be interested in selling them in your restaurant. You can add them to your dessert menu or something."

I look at her in shock. "Denise, you don't just go asking stuff like that."

"Why not? He's a," she makes quotes with her fingers, "friend, isn't he? Don't you want to help your friend out, Jack?" she asks, turning her attention back to him.

He smiles and laughs at the small exchange. "You're right. Kaylan is a good friend, and I want to help her any way I can. Let me run it by Oliver and see what he says. He's a bit of a food snob and not big on desserts, but I'll try my best."

Denise looks content with his answer and she sits back and takes a sip of her coffee. I look at Jack and mouth 'thank you', a smile playing on his lips as he takes a sip of his coffee. "Well, I've got to get back to work. Kaylan, why don't you take off a little early to see if you can convince Jack to accept my offer." I look at her, eyes wide and slightly horror-stricken. I'm not exactly sure how she meant her words to come out, but it was enough to make me turn red as a tomato.

CHAPTER THIRTEEN

*T*he weekend goes by too quickly, but the silver lining is Kevin hasn't come down. He did call, but I told him I need a few more days and basically hung up on him. He continued to call the rest of the weekend, so I shut off my phone. Anyone that needs me can come to find me easily enough. Uncle Rob comes into the shop Monday morning with Dan in tow.

"Morning, Uncle Rob. Hi, Dan. What brings you by?" I ask, looking back and forth between both men.

"Kaylan, Dan has been trying to get in touch with you, but your phone has been off. We all need to talk. Can we go into the office?" Rob asks. His features are soft, but I can see the concern in his eyes.

"How about we go up to the apartment? It will be more comfortable. The office is so small." I look over at Jessica and she shrugs her shoulders. "Jessica, I'll be back. Can you let Denise know in case she's looking for me?" She nods her head and the three of us make our way into the small apartment. "Can I get you anything to drink?" I ask as they take a seat on the couch.

"No, thank you," Rob replies. Dan shakes his head and pulls

some papers out of his briefcase. Rob turns his attention to Dan and pushes a heavy sigh past his lips.

"Kaylan, the shop's not doing well at all. There were a few miscalculations in revenue, and we are actually in the hole more than originally anticipated." He plays with the papers, rolling them between his hands.

"What do you mean, miscalculations?"

"I fumbled a few numbers when I was inputting information around the time of your aunt's death. I caught my mistake a few days ago, and I've been trying to get in touch with you since. When I couldn't, I got in touch with Rob here, and he thought it would be best to wait until today to tell you since nothing was open yesterday anyway. I'm so sorry. I am normally right on point, but I think the sudden news of your aunt's passing caused me to pay less attention to my work."

"How much were you off?" I feel as if I am going to be sick. My stomach is in knots and I swallow the lump in my throat.

"We have enough money in the account for the rest of this month, but after that, we are at a loss. Again, Kaylan, I'm so sorry." He hands the papers to me so I can look at them. Everything on the paper looks like gibberish, none of the numbers meaning anything to me.

"Kaylan," Rob begins, and I look into his eyes. "I told you if this doesn't work out we can look into selling it. It might be time to start looking into that option."

I nod my head and look back at Dan, who looks defeated. "How much is needed to get us into an okay spot for a while longer?"

"You need about five grand to make ends meet for the next month. After that, unless you can drum up a lot of business, you need to look into other options." He pauses and takes a deep breath. "I'm so sorry. I know this isn't what you wanted to hear, and it makes things more difficult."

I gather my thoughts before speaking. "Dan, I know you didn't do this on purpose. No, it's not good news, but I have some money set aside in savings. I can use that to cover the expenses for the month."

"Kaylan, don't do anything that is going to put yourself in a financial bind. If the shop can't stay afloat with the business you currently have, maybe it's time to close up. I know your aunt wouldn't want you to use your savings for this. She wants to see you happy and settle down, get a house and have a family," Rob jumps in.

I rub the hem of my shirt between my fingers. "It's fine. I have a few potential clients that might want to sell some of our stuff in their stores. I'm just waiting to hear back from them." *Lies. No one is calling me back, but I don't want them to know that.* I don't want to have to break the news to Denise or Jessica that they are going to be out of a job soon. I don't want to have to return to the city; I still have a job but no place to stay. The short time I have been here felt more like home than the city with Kevin ever did. I fooled myself into thinking that's where I needed to be. "I'll get the money and get it into the account tomorrow."

I lead the men out and sit in my apartment for a few more minutes, absorbing everything Dan told me. Opening my laptop, I look at the joint account Kevin and I have. I begin the transfer of the money needed for the shop and try to clear my mind before I go back downstairs. No need to worry Denise or Jessica yet. There is still time to correct this, and maybe someone will call back and will be willing to sell our stuff. I am keeping my fingers crossed.

My phone goes off with an incoming text and I open it.

Jack: *Bad news. Oliver doesn't want to sell the desserts. I tried reasoning with him, but he keeps shutting me down. I'll keep at it, but he's as stubborn as an ass sometimes!*

I sigh and hit reply.

Me: *It was sweet of you to even ask. Denise shouldn't have put you on the spot like that. Thank you.*

I let out a frustrated growl and run my hands down my face. Everything is going to shit, and I didn't know how to fix this. I look up at the ceiling and say, "Aunt Sheryl, what did you get me into? I should have just sold this place while I had the chance." I can hear her in my mind telling me that everything is going to be all right, and then she would offer me a cookie to make me feel better. *I wish a cookie would solve all my problems now.*

I head back into the shop and put a smile on my face. Denise basically storms me at the door. "Well, what did he say? Is everything all right?"

"Everything's fine. It's going to be fine," I reply, keeping the smile plastered on my face.

"Is Jack able to help out?"

"I'm not sure, he hasn't gotten back to me yet." I'm lying to everyone so much it's starting to make me dizzy. I'm trying so hard to keep people from stressing out that I'm sure I'm going to give myself an ulcer. "Everything is going to be okay, Denise. I'm taking care of it."

She nods her head and heads back to the kitchen to get the phone. A minute later, she comes back through the door. "Kaylan, the phone's for you." I scurry through the door and pick up the receiver.

"Hello?"

"Kaylan, you need to talk to me."

"Kevin, why the hell are you calling me at work?" I throw my hands up in frustration.

"You wouldn't answer your phone all weekend and we need

to discuss things. I'm on my way down and you *will* talk to me. I want a chance to explain myself. You owe me that."

"I don't owe you shit, Kevin."

"Goddamn it, Kaylan, stop being stubborn for one minute and listen to me. I'm coming to get you and we will go to dinner, that nice place we went to—*Red Bird*. We will talk like civil humans, and at the end of it, if you want to walk away from the life we had then fine. We will finish figuring out how to divide our stuff and you can be done with me."

I am silent, trying to get the words to form. *Screw you, not in a million years,* or *when hell freezes over.* "Okay." It is the only word my lips are able to form, and I feel defeated for uttering the word out loud.

"I'll pick you at six outside the apartment. See you then."

"Fine." I hang up the phone and lean against the wall. This is the last thing I want to deal with tonight. I hope Jack isn't working. I don't want to have to deal with that awkwardness. I think about texting him but decide against it, not wanting to raise any alarms. This is going to be an interesting day, to say the least.

CHAPTER FOURTEEN

I finish closing the shop and head upstairs to take a quick shower before Kevin shows up. Between my other job and the bakery today, I just want to go to sleep for the next twenty years. I'm so worn out and I'm dreading this dinner, but he has a point. I should at least be reasonable and listen to what he has to say. It's only fair. The only problem is, life isn't fair, and I don't want to give him his chance.

I finish getting ready and throw a bit of product in my hair and a hint of make-up on my face. I look at myself in the mirror, settling on a navy sheath dress with ruching in the middle and a sensible pair of nude pumps. I know the restaurant is nicer and want to make sure I look appropriate to go. My phone goes off and I look at it, seeing a text from Kevin letting me know he is downstairs.

He is waiting outside the car for me, by the passenger door. "You look nice, Kaylan," he says as he opens the passenger door for me. Once I am settled, he closes it and hops in on his side.

"Thanks," I reply as he sits.

"Thanks for meeting with me tonight."

"You didn't leave me much of a choice, did you?" I glance over at him from the corner of my eye and see a smile tug at his lips.

"Not really. I wanted to be able to explain everything to you. I don't want us to break up. I love you, Kaylan. You're good for me. How have you been? How's the shop?"

I think about how to answer. Do I tell him the store is in trouble? Do I tell him everything is fine? I guess he's going to find out soon enough when he sees the money has been transferred from our account.

"I'm fine, but the store isn't doing too well. It's been hard since Sheryl passed away, and business has been slow."

Gripping the steering wheel tighter, he replies quietly, "Sorry to hear that. Are you going to sell it and come back to the city?"

I shrug my shoulders. "I don't know yet."

"You can always come home. Didn't your uncle say if it wasn't working you could sell it? I think it's time for that."

I don't respond and look out the window instead. A few minutes pass, and he pulls into the parking lot of the restaurant. When he puts it in park, I all but jump out of the car and begin walking toward the front door, not even waiting for him. Kevin's legs are much longer than mine, though, and he catches up quickly. He tries to take my hand, but I pull it out of his grip. He lets out a frustrated sigh but doesn't try again.

We are led to our table by the friendly hostess, and Kevin orders a bottle of wine for the table along with our meals. I pick up my glass and down half of it right away. Kevin cocks his eyebrow and looks at me. "Thirsty?"

"I figure it will be easier to listen if I have a bit of a buzz," I deadpan. I look around the restaurant for Jack; I don't want him to see me with Kevin tonight. "We're here, Kevin, so please explain to me how things are not what they seemed."

"Theresa is a friend from work. We were both having a rough time, and I let her stay at the apartment for a little while so I'd have some company. It was hard for me when you left to do this. Then we began talking less and less and you were always so busy. I felt like I didn't matter to you anymore."

I can't believe *that* is the excuse he is giving me. I want to yell at him so bad, remind him that this is no picnic for me either. Remind him *I* am working two jobs, getting up early to be in the shop to bake at four in the morning. I feel a sinister smile spread across my face. I know I said I didn't want to know, but now I feel as if I'll bust if I don't. "Kevin, will you answer a question honestly for me?"

He swallows hard, and I watch his Adam's apple bobbing up and down. "Sure."

"How long have you been fucking her?"

"I didn't mean for it to happen. I want you to know that."

"How long?" I ask again through clenched teeth.

"It was only a few times and we'd both had too much to drink. I don't feel anything for her, not like what I feel for you. You know me and where I'm coming from; you understand me."

He stops talking as the waitress comes by with our food. We both thank her politely and I turn my harsh gaze back to him, waiting. He looks down at his food and begins digging in, ignoring my stare. I push my plate away from me and grab my glass of wine, downing the rest of the contents and pouring more.

"Aren't you going to eat?" he asks, motioning toward my plate with his fork.

"I'm not hungry. Are you going to answer my *actual* question?"

"Not as long as you think."

What the hell kind of answer was that? "So, before or after you broke up with me?"

"Technically after."

"Glad to know there's a technicality in there."

He looks past me, waves at someone and smiles. I turn my

head and see it's Jack. When he meets my eyes, his warm expression changes and his smile fades. *Fuck.* I'm not doing anything wrong by having dinner, but I want to tell him about this later. He walks over to our table.

"Hello, Kaylan." He looks at me and then turns his attention to Kevin. "Kevin. How are you enjoying dinner this evening?" His demeanor is professional, but I can hear the annoyance dancing in his voice.

"Dinner is great. Food is just as good as I remember it, thanks. I have a question for you, Jack. When did you start sleeping with my girlfriend?"

"Kevin," I warn. "Jack has nothing to do with this."

"I don't think you're innocent in any of this either, Kaylan." His voice turns bitter and harsh.

"Why are you causing a scene? Are you drunk?" I whisper-yell at him. He shrugs his shoulders, not giving an answer.

Jack smiles and pulls a chair up so the back is resting against the table, and sits down, legs spread open. He rests his arms over the top of the chair. "Kevin, I'm going to ask you nicely to not cause a scene in my restaurant. Also, that's really none of your business."

Kevin puts his hands up in defense. "It's a simple question, Jack. I saw how you looked at her when I first met you. You've been dying to get your hands on her since then. So, when did you *fuck* Kaylan? Was it after we broke up? Was it before?" He turns and looks at me. "Was it after I left that first weekend?"

I feel the tears stinging my eyes. "Kevin, stop this. Jealousy is not a good look for you."

He throws his napkin on the table and stands, causing my glass of wine to spill. I jump up quickly to avoid the red liquid but am unsuccessful, a small amount landing on my dress. "You're getting fat anyway. Enjoy her, Jack." He walks toward the exit, his words stinging my ears.

Jack jumps up from his seat. "Hey, Kevin, you forgot something." His voice is calm, but it burns with rage.

He turns toward Jack just in time for his fist to meet his face. Everyone is watching the events and a few groans can be heard amongst the spectators. I look on in horror as Kevin goes down hard and Jack cradles his fist with his other hand. "Don't ever come back here. I'll do more than break your nose next time." He walks to one of his wait staff and says something to him quietly, then turns to look at me. "Come on." Grabbing my hand, he practically drags me toward the kitchen.

"What the fuck is going on out there, Jack?" a man asks as we enter the kitchen.

"Some drunk asshole got unruly and I punched him. Fuck, that hurt." He murmurs the last part as he shakes out his hand. He grabs a towel and puts some ice from the chest freezer in it, placing the cold bag over his right hand.

"You punched someone, Jack?"

"Not now, Oliver. I'll take care of it, just give me a few minutes."

"Who's the girl?" Oliver asks, noticing me standing behind Jack.

"The girl I was defending. This is Kaylan. Kaylan, this is Oliver, my business partner."

I wave at him. "Nice to meet you."

He apprises me for a moment. "You too." Turning his attention back to Jack, he states, "It better have been worth it, Jack."

"You have no fucking idea." He ushers me into the back office and closes the door. "Sit." I sit down, nerves shot from everything I just witnessed. He kneels down in front of me. "Are you okay?" He tucks my hair behind my ear, his kind blue eyes looking directly into mine.

"Yes," I whisper. "I'm okay."

"Why didn't you tell me you were coming with him tonight?"

"He wanted a chance to explain, and I wanted to just get this done and over with so I could be done with him. I thought it wouldn't matter if I told you tomorrow. I didn't want you to try to talk me out of it, because I needed closure so I could move on."

"I wouldn't have talked you out of it. I actually would like if you were done with him entirely. It gives us a chance to make things work. I'm sorry about what happened, and he shouldn't have said that to you. You're not fat; he's just jealous that he lost you. He's an idiot."

I focus my attention on the stain on my dress and run my fingers over it. "I should get home. I'm so sorry about how everything escalated tonight. I'll call an Uber or something. I came here with him."

"Let me take care of the mess I made out front and then I'll take you home. Can you give me thirty minutes or so?"

"That's sweet of you, but you don't have to do that."

"Kaylan, please, I need to make sure you get home safe." His tone leaves no room for discussion. I reach my hand out and cradle his cheek in my palm. He leans into the embrace and turns his head to plant a small kiss in the center of it.

"Okay."

He leans forward and presses his lips against mine. Placing my hand on his chest, I can feel his heart beating like crazy and I pull him in closer, needing to feel him. His lips are soft and needy against mine, and I moan as he deepens the kiss.

He pulls back reluctantly. "I'll be back. Stay here."

CHAPTER FIFTEEN

*I*t takes him a bit longer to talk to all the patrons than he originally thought. A few people complain, but most of them congratulate him for what he did. The few people that did complain, he comped their meal and apologized profusely, which appeased them. When he came to get me, I had fallen asleep with my head on my arm on the desk.

"Kaylan, babe, wake up," he says quietly as he rubs my back. I groan and sit up, looking at him through red puffy eyes. He helps me stand and pulls me into a tight embrace, his body helping to put mine at ease.

"I don't want to go back to my place tonight. Can I stay with you?"

"Sure. I had Oliver whip up something for us. I know you probably aren't hungry after everything, but you should try to eat something." We walk out of the office and Jack takes the bag from Oliver.

I look toward Oliver. "Sorry about tonight. I didn't know that would happen."

He shrugs his shoulders. "Shit happens. Jack said it didn't

affect too many people. Next time, maybe don't bring him back though, huh?" He smiles, amused by the situation at hand.

"Yeah, you don't have to worry about that. Thanks for understanding."

The ride to Jack's is silent. I'm wrapped up in my own thoughts. He keeps glancing over at me, but I refuse to look his way. When we pull into his driveway, he turns off the engine. "Say something, Kaylan, please." He sounds angry, but I know it's not at me.

"What do you want me to say?" My voice is raw from holding back tears for so long.

"Anything, I don't care. Yell. Scream. Cry. Do anything but sit there silently. You sitting here like this, not saying anything, is killing me. At least, if you talk, I can figure out how to make things better."

"There's nothing to say. He was a dick. He never used to be that way, you know." I turn to look at him, my eyes shimmering. "He used to look at me and talk to me like I was the most amazing person he had ever met. Even when we first got together and I had a little extra weight, he never said anything, never talked bad about me; he only ever showed me love. I guess, when he got a new job, he started changing. I didn't want to see it happening. I worked hard to keep my weight in check so I could be the girl he wanted."

"How long ago did he get a new job?"

"About a year ago." I stop and think about it. There were a few signs that he was changing, but I overlooked them as stress from the job. He started working longer hours and I was left alone more and more. He helped me set up a gym schedule and checked in to make sure I completed workouts, kept me away from my aunt and uncle more and more. The list goes on and on. I let out a strangled sob and cover my mouth.

"Kaylan, let's get inside so we can lay down." He gets out and opens my door, leading me into the house. I kick off my heels and follow him toward the bedroom. After he helps me into a t-shirt and an oversized pair of shorts, we lay down and he curls his body around mine, protecting me. The tears fall and he holds me tighter, whispering soothing words in my ear. "It's okay, I'm here."

We stay together like that for some time, my body shaking from silently crying. At some point, I doze off, and when I wake up a few hours later, Jack isn't there. I get up and walk into the kitchen, where he is eating food and talking on the phone quietly.

"Thank you, I appreciate it." He turns and sees I'm standing there. "Hey, I've gotta go. Thank you again. Please let me know as soon as you do." He hangs up the phone and offers a small smile in my direction. "Want something to eat?" I nod and he gets another plate out, putting some food on it and popping it in the microwave.

"Who was that?" I take a seat at the table and pull my foot under my leg.

"Just a friend, seeing if she can help me out with something."

He carries the plate over, along with some utensils, and I dig in. It's roast chicken, with rosemary potatoes, and lemon broccoli. It tastes delicious, and I'm glad I decided to eat something, even though food is the last thing on my mind. "What time is it?"

"Almost ten-thirty." He sits in the chair next to me, holding my gaze. You slept for a few hours, but my stomach was rumbling and I needed to eat," he says sheepishly.

I take a few more bites and push the plate away from me. "I'm done."

"Kaylan, you hardly ate anything. Please take a few more bites."

"I'm not in the mood for food after all. I have too much on my mind right now. I appreciate you letting me crash here for the night. I do have to leave in a few hours to get home though. You could always drive me home now if you prefer so you don't have to get up so early."

"Nope, I want you in my bed tonight. I want to be able to wrap my arms around you and kiss you. I'll make sure the alarm is set, and I'll get you to the shop in time."

"Thank you, Jack, for everything. You're being really wonderful through all of this, and I feel like I don't deserve it."

"Kaylan, I've wanted to get to know you for a long time now. I'm glad I'm getting the chance to. Don't say you don't deserve my affections, because you do. You're good for me. Trust me when I say you're doing more for me than I am for you." He collects his thoughts, and it seems he's waging an inner war with himself. Finally, his eyes meet mine. "Can I ask you a favor?"

"Anything. You've helped me so much."

"Would you have dinner with me and my parents this weekend? Before you say yes, though, my dad can be kind of a dick and he's the reason I haven't been in contact with my mom for a while. My mom called me the other day and told me Dad's sick. She asked me to try and talk to him. I'm doing this for her because I know how important it is, but I don't think I can go and handle it alone."

"I'd love to meet them."

"Great. Another thing," he takes a deep breath before continuing, "I told Mom I was going to bring you, and she got the scoop from Steph. I'm not exactly sure what Steph said, but Mom seemed very excited that I wanted to bring you to meet them. I'm sorry in advance for whatever happens."

I smile and tease, "What if I said no and didn't want to come?"

"Can't take it back now, you already agreed. I am sorry, though, for all the questions I'm sure she will throw at you. I did explain that you were just a friend, but I don't think she bought it."

Fidgeting and looking at the table, I ask, "What if I wanted to be more than that?"

When I look back up to meet his eyes, they are sparkling and he looks so happy. "If you wanted that, you would make me very happy. I'd like that, too, but I haven't wanted to pressure you into anything."

"Well, are you going to ask me?"

His smile lights up his face. "Kaylan, will you be my girlfriend?"

I move to his lap and kiss him on the lips, and he opens immediately to give me more access to his mouth. His hands curl through my hair, and he keeps me in place as he tastes me. I press my body into his, needing to feel more and I wrap my arms around his neck. I let out a small whimper as he breaks the kiss. "Why'd you stop?" I ask, my breathing heavy.

He presses his forehead to mine. "I'm waiting for my answer."

"Yes," I whisper, and he kisses me again.

CHAPTER SIXTEEN

*T*he alarm goes off, and I begrudgingly drag myself away from Jack, the cool air hitting my naked body sending shivers through me. I turn to look at him and he looks back up at me sleepily.

"Good morning to my beautiful girlfriend. Are you sure you have to get up? We could play hooky from work, stay in bed," he smirks, "explore each other some more?" He cocks his eyebrow and his eyes darken, lust taking over.

"As wonderful as that sounds, I need to get to the shop and try to turn things around. If not, I'm looking at having to sell it." I put on my bra and pull my dress on, trying to return to some modesty.

"If you have to sell, what are you planning on doing? You can't go back to your apartment with Kevin." He sits up and throws a shirt and shorts on as well, getting ready to drive me back to my apartment.

"No. I don't know what I'm going to do, maybe stay with my girlfriend Katie. I'm sure she would let me crash there. My job won't allow me to do remote work forever, and the city is where the rest of my life is. My job, my friends..." I trail off.

"What about me?" he asks, his voice soft as he stands directly in front of me.

I look at him and place my hand on his cheek, a tired smile on my lips. "I don't know yet. Let's not think of that right now. Who knows? Maybe in another week or so, my luck will change and the shop will begin doing well. We will figure it all out. Until then, let's just enjoy our time." I stand on my toes, give him a small kiss on the cheek, and grab my purse so we can leave.

The ride to the shop is quick, and the two of us head up into my apartment so I can change before heading downstairs. I come out of my room in an oversized t-shirt and workout pants. He looks at me with a slight smile gracing his lips. "What's with the baggy clothes?"

"I'm behind on laundry, and I'm coming down to bare bones of clothing. I have to do some today. I just don't want to haul everything to the laundromat. I guess I don't have much of an option though, huh?" I ask as I hold out the shirt and look down at my wardrobe choice.

"You could always wear one of the black t-shirts that were left here."

I narrow my eyes and look at him. "How did you know about those?"

"You, uh, you mentioned some guy's clothes were left here. You offered some of them to me when I stayed over that first night, remember?" His hand flies to his hair and he tussles it as he looks around the room. *Did I show him those shirts? If so, why does he remember that?*

"Feel free to make yourself at home if you want, but I'm sure you want to go back to bed for a bit. You haven't had much sleep and I know this is very early for you."

"No, I think I'm going to head out. If you want you can stay over tonight and do your laundry at my house. I don't mind."

I laugh. "We really won't have secrets if I do my laundry over there. You don't need to see my comfy granny panties. I've kept those hidden from you for a reason."

He laughs as we leave the apartment and I lock up. At the bottom of the stairs, he gives me a kiss goodbye and I unlock the shop to begin my day. I watch from inside as he hops into his car and pulls away, waving at me as he goes.

I walk into the kitchen and my phone goes off with an incoming text. Pulling it from my pocket, I see it's from Kevin. "Ugh, what the hell does he want?" I mumble and open the text.

> Kevin: *You moved $5000 over from our account for your fucking escapade? You're an idiot if you think that will keep it going. The shop is going to close and you're going to be out almost all your savings.*

> Me: *Well, it's not exactly your concern anymore, is it? It's my money and I'll do what I want with it. I am coming by this week to get the rest of my stuff, and you'd better not be there when I do. I'll make sure it's during the day so I don't interrupt your evening activities.*

> Kevin: *Have fun with the screw-up. Hope you know what you're getting into. I've done some research on this guy, and let me tell you, he's not all he's cracked up to be.*

I feel my blood boil, and I want to scream at him. He knows nothing of Jack and has no right to interfere with my life or my choices.

Me: *It's a good thing that's none of your concern either then.*

I close my phone and prep everything to begin baking or the day. Denise walks in a few minutes later.

"What's up, buttercup? You look like you've had a rough night. Are you okay?" she asks, putting her purse in the office and slipping an apron over her head.

"Yeah, just had a crappy night, and Kevin is texting me so I'm annoyed. Don't mind me," I say, starting to cream butter and sugar in the mixer.

"If you want to talk, I'm more than happy to listen; although, I think you make a better couple with Jack, if you want my opinion." She goes about her business, pretending she didn't say anything of the sort. We work in silence with only the radio keeping us company for most of the morning. She asks a question here and there, but I'm really not in a talking mood.

Jessica comes in just before the shop opens, and I see Jack outside by his car on the phone. "I'll be right back," I say as I walk outside. I cross the street to Jack and hear him deep in conversation. He sees me walking toward him and ends the call before I can reach him. He smiles and leans down to give me a gentle kiss.

"Yum, sugar and chocolate, my favorite flavor for you." He licks his lips and hands a coffee to me. "So, I thought I would come by and get your laundry in the car, and then maybe in a little bit, we can go for a run or something?"

I take a sip of my steaming drink and sigh as the hot liquid travels down my throat. "I've got a better idea. I need to get the rest of my stuff out of my apartment. There are a couple of small pieces of furniture and a nice piece of artwork that are mine. I would really like to get them out of there. Since your car is a bit bigger than mine, think you could help me? It should fit in your Jeep."

"Sure, what time do you want to go?"

"The sooner the better. I need to be finished with him. We will still have to sort out the lease, but that can be a different day. For now, I would like knowing *all* my stuff is out of that apartment and I won't have to see him again.

"Let me go fill up with gas and I'll come back. We can be ready to go whenever you need."

"Thank you, Jack. You go out of your way for me, and I truly appreciate you for it. It's very sweet."

"Oh, didn't I tell you that you are paying me for this?" He smirks.

"Oh yeah? What kind of payment do you require?"

He bends down so his lips press against my ear and whispers, "Give me a few éclairs and a few nights where you allow me to have you any way I want and we'll call it even."

I shiver thinking about me and him in bed and the fun we could be having. "Well, if that's all it takes, I should have you do me favors all the time."

THE TRIP to the city is quick, and we are able to get into the apartment without any issues. I unlock the door and look around. The place is a pit. I scrunch my face in disgust and shake my head before letting out a small sigh. I just hope he didn't do anything to my stuff.

"Wow, this place is a pit," Jack comments as he looks around.

"He's always been so clean. This isn't normal, but it's how it was last time I was here, too. Come on, let's get my stuff and get out of here." We walk into the office and take my painting off the wall. It was my mother's favorite, a seascape. Thank goodness it's not damaged. Jack takes it from me and places it over by the front door, then we walk into the bedroom. This room is worse than the rest of the apartment. The bed is disheveled and clothes are thrown all over the room.

I open my nightstand and grab my few personal belongings from it then grab the lamp as well. Moving around the room, trying to not disturb anything, I can sense Jack is uncomfortable. I turn to look at him and see his hands are in fists by his sides. "Can you take this into the living room?" I hold out the lamp for him. "And get the stacking tables, too? Those are mine as well. I have a few more items to collect in here and then we can go. I'll sort out the lease with the landlord later." He nods his head and leaves the room without saying anything else.

"Kay, can you come here?" he asks.

I throw the other few items in a bag and walk into the living room, my eyes following his line of vision. In bright red lipstick, the word *Bitch* is scribbled on the top table. I lick my lips and nod my head before turning toward the kitchen to get a towel and clean it up. "Can you take these other items down to the car? I'll clean this up and then we can head out." I keep my voice calm, but my heart is hammering out of my chest; I want to scream. Good thing it is only lipstick and it will come off easily enough. The bad news is it is probably my lipstick. I left some make-up here, figuring I wouldn't need it, but I refuse to take it with me now.

I finish cleaning the table and look at the others, making sure they're fine. They seem to be, so I pick up the tables and move them toward the door. Jack comes back up and looks at me, asking a silent question.

"They're fine, I got the lipstick off. Can you load them up as well? I'll be down in a few minutes so you can wait there."

He picks all three up and carries them down the stairs. I take one more look around, making sure I have everything that belongs to me, and then wave bye to my former apartment.

Jack is leaning against the side of his Jeep when I come down with a small bag thrown over my shoulder. I open the back door, put it in with the rest of my stuff, and take a deep breath.

"You okay?" he asks, his hand on the small of my back.

I turn to look at him and give a small smile. "Yeah, I'm okay. Break-ups are never easy anyway. At least I didn't have to see him today, and now I'm done with him." He pulls me into a hug and then helps me into the Jeep. I look up at the building as we are leaving, giving silent thanks that Kevin didn't come around.

CHAPTER SEVENTEEN

I finalize everything with the housing office and get my name taken off the lease. I mail my key back to Kevin with a note that lets him know if he tries to contact me again, I'll get a restraining order against him. I'm thankful he hasn't messaged me or tried to contact me yet, and I hope that continues.

Jack and I begin spending every night together, either at my place or his. If I stay at his house, I drive so he can sleep in in the mornings. He usually gets up to walk me out and then returns to his bed for a few more hours of sleep. We have fallen into an easy routine over the past few days, and I am happy to have him.

The rest of the week goes by in a blur, and we are getting ready to go to dinner at his parents' house. I put on a multicolored t-shirt dress and accent it with a chunky belt, a light sweater, and a pair of cute, strappy, flat sandals. After pulling my hair back into a low bun, I finish with a splash of make-up. Jack is going to be here any minute, and I need to pack the cookies I decided to bake for dessert. The buzzer goes off and I let him up.

"Hey, gorgeous, are you ready to go?" he asks as he opens the door and looks at me in the kitchen.

"Yep, just give me a minute. I need to get the rest of these cookies on a tray and get them wrapped."

"You made cookies to bring? You didn't have to do that," he comments as he walks up behind me.

"I was always taught never to arrive empty-handed, so I figure since I own a bakery, why not bake something for dessert?" I turn my head to the side so he can kiss my cheek.

"Always so thoughtful. Mom will love it. Thank you." He kisses my neck and his fingers dance over my stomach, sending a rush of heat between my legs. A small moan passes my lips and I press back into him. His chuckle pulls me back to reality. "I wish we had time, babe. You always feel so good wrapped around me, but I don't want to be late. I promise, tonight, I'm all yours." He pulls away and leaves me standing there all hot and bothered as I try to wrap the cookies.

He doesn't live far from his parents, so it's a surprise to me that he doesn't see them that often; or at least his mom since he's not on good terms with his dad. We pull into the driveway and I look at Jack. His hands are gripping the steering wheel tightly, and he lets out a shaky breath. The issue with his dad must be bad if he is this nervous to be here. I place my hand on his thigh and give him a reassuring squeeze. "It's going to be fine."

His eyes lock with mine, and he leans over in a swift motion, capturing my lips with his. His hands frame my face, holding me in place, and I grab his wrists to grip onto something. He licks the seam of my lips, coaxing them open, and slips his tongue in my mouth. I'm panting, needing so much more than this, but now is not the time. I pull my head back and look at him. His pupils are dilated and his breathing is ragged. "It's not too late to go back. I'll have you for dinner." He smirks.

"It *is* too late." I point toward the woman running out of the house. "Looks like your mom knows we're here."

He groans and gets out of the car. I slip out my side and grab Jack's arm, and he takes the cookies from me. We meet her halfway up the driveway; her smile is infectious and she is practically giggling. This woman is shorter than me, somewhere around five-foot-nothing, with greying blonde hair and the same blue eyes as Jack.

"There's my favorite son!" She pulls him down into a hug and plants a kiss on his cheek. I drop my arm so he can hug her back. She pulls back reluctantly and smiles at me. "You must be Kaylan. I've heard so much about you. I'm so happy to meet you finally. I'm Jane." She pulls me in for a hug.

"It's nice to meet you, too. Thank you so much for the invitation tonight. I baked some cookies for dessert."

"That's so sweet of you. Thank you so much." She takes the tray of cookies from Jack and motions for us to follow her. "Come on, don't want you two standing out here all night. Come inside."

I feel Jack tense beside me, and I place a reassuring hand on his arm. He looks down at me and gives me a small smile, letting me know he is going to be all right. We walk into the house, and I look around as his mom carries the cookies into the kitchen. "Can I get you kids something to drink?" she calls out.

"I'll have a beer, and if you've got any wine for Kaylan, that would be great," Jack responds, moving closer to the kitchen. She comes back with our drinks and Jack is looking around. "Where's Dad?"

"He ran out to the store. He should be back in a few minutes. It's a nice night out, so I thought we could sit on the back deck for dinner. Is that all right with you guys?"

Jack looks at me in question. I smile and nod my head. He looks back at his mom. "Sounds good. I'm going to give Kaylan a tour of the house. We'll be back soon."

"Sure, honey. Don't take too long. I don't get to see you that often, and I want to get as much time in with you as I can."

He takes my hand and shows me around downstairs first—the kitchen, formal dining room, and then the living room. Each room is decorated minimally, with a few pieces of artwork on the walls and a few pieces of furniture. When we walk into the living room, it is a different story entirely. The walls are covered in family photos. I can tell, when he was younger, they were a close family. I remember Jack telling me his dad was in the Army and they traveled a lot, and these pictures tell the same story. Mostly, they're pictures of his mom and him in front of different national landmarks. There are a few of him alone with a big smile plastered on his face and even a few with his dad.

I lean in closer to examine one of the photos of the three of them. Jack looks so much like his father, it's eerie. He has the same shape of face, hair color, and smile, but he has his mother's soft and caring eyes.

"You look so much like him," I comment as I point to the picture.

"Yeah, so I've been told." He takes a sip of his beer, his nerves getting to him.

"How about you show me your old bedroom, huh?" I ask, wiggling my eyebrows, trying to ease some of his tension. He smiles and a small chuckle passes his lips as he takes my hand and leads me upstairs. At the end of the hallway, he pushes open the bedroom door and ushers me inside, closing the door quietly behind him.

"This is it." He gestures around the room, allowing me to look at the trophies and knickknacks on the shelf. He has a giant poster of Britney Spears next to his bed, and I point to it and laugh.

"Guess she was your wet dream, huh? Is there a guy out there that didn't have a thing for Britney?" I take a sip of my wine, and he wraps his arms around my waist, his lips grazing my ear.

"You're my wet dream, baby. Don't you forget it." I feel myself get wet and I tilt my head to the side to give him more access to my neck. "I can be super fast if you can be quiet. I'll make it up to you later, but I need something to take the edge off of seeing my dad. Please." He is practically begging. The thrill of doing it in his bedroom sends a wave of pleasure and excitement rolling through me, but I'm holding back, not wanting to get caught.

He reaches up and pinches my nipple, and I arch my back, a whimper leaving my lips. "Please, Kaylan. I can't be drunk when I see him, but I'm freaking out here."

"You owe me an explanation after tonight as to why you're at odds with him." I place my hands on the end of his bed and press my ass back into him. I hear him undo his belt buckle and unzip his pants, pulling them down. He flips my dress up and pulls my panties down my legs. I step out of them and spread my legs, giving him enough access.

"Baby, I'll tell you whatever you need to know," he whispers as he presses into me slowly, both of us groaning quietly. He snaps his hips back and forth. I reach my hand down and start rubbing my clit quickly, my fingers knocking against his cock in the process. "Fuck, Kay, just like that. I can feel you squeezing me."

"Harder, Jack. You feel so good." His cock is hitting the sweet spot inside me and I'm getting closer with each thrust. "Oh, fuck," I moan, my orgasm hitting me suddenly. He continues to thrust, the sounds of our bodies echoing through his small room only prolonging my euphoric high. I feel him swell in me and finally release, coming with a groan.

His hand is on the small of my back as he catches his breath. He reaches behind him for a few tissues and hands some to me to help clean up some of the mess. I pull my panties back into place and turn to face him. "Is my hair and make-up still okay?"

He smooths a few stray strands down and gives me a kiss on the lips. "You look perfect. Thank you, Kaylan. I know that's not what you imagined happening, and neither did I." He rakes his hands through his hair, tousling it a bit. "He just makes me so crazy." We hear a car pull into the driveway and look out the window. A salt-and-pepper-haired man gets out carrying a brown bag. "That's him. We should go."

As we make our way down the stairs, Jack keeps me behind his body, and he stops, locking eyes with the man coming through the door. "Hi, Dad," he says quietly.

"Jane, what's he doing here?" he asks, anger lacing his voice.

"Fred, you promised you would behave today. I told you he was coming to dinner with his girlfriend," she warns.

I poke my head out from behind Jack and give a small wave. "Hello, Mr. Madison, it's a pleasure to meet you. My name's Kaylan." I move out from behind Jack and extend my hand for him to shake. He looks at it, looks back at Jack, and finally takes it.

"Nice to meet you. Call me Fred," he mumbles.

I know it's going to take a lot to win this man over, so I put a smile on my face, trying to stay as positive and happy as I can. "Jane, Fred," I look between the two of them, "you have a lovely home. Is there anything I can do to help with dinner?"

"Oh, no, dear, everything is ready to go. We can do sit outside and relax. I just need Fred to fire up the grill and cook the meat. You do eat meat, right?" Shock strikes her features. "I didn't even think to ask."

I give a light giggle. "Yes, I eat meat. It's fine. I'm not a picky eater."

"Perfect. Well then, follow me and you can tell me all about my son since I never get to see him." She gives a death stare to

Fred, and we all follow her outside and take seats around the table.

The meal is perfect. Everyone is pleasant, and Jane looks so happy to have her son at home. I help her clean up, and we leave the men outside to talk. I peer out the window, and they seem to be in a heated discussion. Trying to ease the tension, I carry the cookies outside. "Would anyone care for a cookie? I made them this morning." I place the tray on the table and sit next to Jack, taking his hand in mine.

Fred reaches for one and takes a bite of it. "Thanks. What kind are these?"

"They're my favorite, chocolate chunk."

"There was a bakery that used to make these all the time. These taste just like them." He takes another bite and offers a small smile.

"*Little Sweet Shoppe*. My Aunt Sheryl used to own the shop, and she made them often. I took over when she passed away a few months ago."

"Sorry for your loss." He looks back at Jack. "At least this one bakes instead of getting baked."

"Dad, now is not the time for that." He's tense, his jaw clenched.

Fred sits forward in his seat, leaning closer to us. "Did Jack tell you about his ex, Monica? Did he tell you how he fucked up his life all for her?"

Looking at Fred, I can tell he has had one too many drinks and he is just going to keep going. Now's the time to play it cool or risk someone flying off the handle. I take a deep breath to calm my nerves. "I know they had a good reason to break up, and that he went through a rough patch that my aunt helped him through. She gave him a job and helped him get his life back on track."

We look toward the door as Jane comes back through with

coffee and mugs. She looks at Fred and Jack, horror written on her face. "Fred, you promised me."

"You should be very proud of your son. He runs a wonderful restaurant and is a generous and giving man. He has a house, a girlfriend that loves him very much, and he means so much to a lot of us. I'm sorry that you can't see past what he's done to see what a wonderful man he is now." I turn toward Jane. "This has been a lovely evening, and I'm sorry to cut it short. I have an early morning tomorrow, and we really should get going. Please come by the shop anytime and I'll get something special for you on the house." I turn back toward Fred. "It was a pleasure meeting you as well, and I hope we will be able to talk again soon. I meant what I said. Your son is a good man and you should be proud of him. Jane, will you walk us out please?"

I stand and take Jack's hand, making him move toward the door with me, his mom right behind us. The three of us stand in the driveway, and she gives Jack a long hug. I allow them a private moment and turn my back, looking toward the car. Jack places his hand on my shoulder, and I turn, looking at both of them. Jane pulls me into a hug and whispers, "I'm so sorry about Fred. Thank you though. You're good for him. Please treat him well."

"He's good for me, too." We pull back and look at one another. "I'm serious about stopping by. Jack comes in every day for an éclair. The two of you can catch up in the shop."

She nods her head, and Jack gives her another hug. "Love you, Mom." He places his hand on the small of my back and leads me to the car. Once he's settled and we are on our way, I turn to look at him. "You've got some explaining to do, mister."

WE ARE LYING IN BED. Jack has made the night up to me by

giving me one orgasm after another. I feel completely boneless, a smile plastered on my face. "Don't think you've tricked me into not asking questions about your dad and your ex. Talk." He remains quiet, looking up at the ceiling, and I place my hand on his bare chest. "Please, Jack, I'm not going to judge you for your past. Whoever you were then, is not who you are now."

He turns his head and looks at me. "I dated Monica for three years. During that time, I was trying to open a restaurant and she was working in a hair salon. We started off really good together, but after about two years, things started to change. She would come home high, sometimes drunk. I used a lot of money that was set aside for the restaurant to get her out of binds. There were a few times she was locked up, and I paid the bail for her. Each and every time, she promised it was the last." He lets out a disgusted laugh. "Last time, right?

"Anyway, she would get better and do well for a few weeks, and then we would be right back where we started. I became good friends with the guys down at the precinct, and they told me if she was ever caught with the stuff, she was going to do time. I loved her, and I didn't want to see that happen to her, so when they came with a warrant to search the house and they found her stash, I lied and said it was mine."

"What was it that she had?"

"She had some pot and some narcotics. I'm not entirely sure. She watched them cart me off and didn't say a word about it. I served a few months jail time for it, but during the few months I was gone, Oliver couldn't keep the place running and the bank didn't want to work with an ex-con."

"What happened to Monica?"

"She skipped town with her drug dealer, I'm assuming. That's when Dad disowned me and made Mom stop talking to me. I've had minimal interaction with her over the past few years, but I'm hoping to change that now that Dad is sick."

"Jack, I'm so sorry that happened. Now, I understand the reference about Monica your dad used tonight." I place a kiss on his chest just above his heart and snuggle down into him.

"Yeah, I'm sorry about tonight. He was an ass and shouldn't have said anything like that to you. It's really none of his business, and it wasn't right of him to bring it up. Mom loved you, though, so you won her over. Dad will come around eventually."

"I like her, too. She's a great lady and she raised a great son."

He scratches his stubbly chin. "Something's been bugging me since you said it earlier, and I hoped you could answer it for me."

"What's that?"

"You said you love me. Do you?"

I adjust my body so I can look into his eyes and smile. "Yeah, I think I do."

He smiles brightly. "I love you, too, Kaylan."

CHAPTER EIGHTEEN

*D*an has been keeping me in the loop with the finances, but things aren't looking good at all. Sales over the past several weeks haven't gotten any better. We will only be able to keep the place going for the next month, and then the reserves are going to be gone. Even with the money I used from my savings, it looks like I am going to have to sell the place.

I walk into the bank with my head held high, wearing a black pencil skirt, dark purple blouse, and a pair of low black pumps. I want to be as professional as possible to help appeal to their better judgment.

"Good morning, I have an appointment with Mrs. Mendes," I say politely to the woman at the table.

"Please have a seat and she will be with you in a few moments."

I take a seat and look around the bank. There are very few customers inside, and a few of the tellers are talking about their evening plans when I hear a few girls giggle. I focus my attention back on the reason I am here and take a few deep breaths to calm my nerves.

"Ms. Santine?"

I look up at a dark-haired woman with a pleasant smile. "Yes." I stand and walk over toward her.

"I'm Diane Mendes." We shake hands and exchange pleasantries. "Please follow me this way." She leads me into her office and closes the door behind her, motioning for me to take a seat. "Now, you are here to discuss your loan for *The Sweet Shoppe,* correct?"

"Yes. I would like to figure out what options I have in regards to keeping the business. Is there any type of refinancing options or a way to defer the loan for a few months?"

"Well, let's pull up the account and take a look at what we are dealing with." She begins typing away on her computer, passing along small talk as she pulls up the information. "Your shop makes the best cake pops out there. Whenever I'm nearby, I stop to get one."

"Thank you. It's a good stress reliever to make them, too," I respond as I think about squishing my hands through the goop while making the balls.

"All right, I have the information here. For a business loan, we don't have any options for refinancing. The only way to go that route would be to switch your loan elsewhere. That is always a possibility, but since we have held this loan for so long, the chances of you getting a better rate are slim. You are welcome to look into it though. As far as deferring, it looks like this loan was deferred two years ago for a few months. We only allow one deferment on the life of the loan. I'm really sorry." She looks at me with pity, and I know she feels bad for dropping the bomb on me.

I look down at my hands and take another deep breath, picking at an invisible piece of lint on my skirt. "Is there anything I can do to keep it going? Do you have any advice for me?"

"I'm not really sure what to tell you. From the standpoint of the loan, it looks like the only way would be to sell the shop and pay off the loan that way. Or, again, you could always see if there is another bank that you could refinance through."

I stand up and stick my hand out toward her. "Thank you so much for your time this morning, Mrs. Mendes. I appreciate it." I turn and walk out of her office, determined not to cry in front of strangers. I have to talk to my uncle and Dan, and then I have to talk to Jessica and Denise. I feel like I am going to be sick, I am so upset. I call Dan and ask if he can meet me at Rob's house, and he agrees to be there within an hour.

On the ride over, I gather my thoughts and try to figure out what I am going to say, how I am going to go about this. I need to find out who I have to contact and what needs to be done to start the sale of the bakery. I don't want to admit it, but I guess it really is time to bring it to an end. My thoughts drift to Jack, and I start thinking about what I'm going to tell him and how we would handle a long-distance relationship. Without the shop, my job is in the city, and I don't think Nancy will let me work remote forever. *Everything is a mess!*

When I pull into the driveway and walk up to the front door, Rob is there waiting for me. "Didn't go so well today, huh?" he asks as he pushes open the door to let me in.

"Nope. I think it's time to close *The Sweet Shoppe*. I'm so sorry, Uncle Rob. I know you really wanted me to try, but this is such a mess. Sales aren't where they should be. I looked into different avenues as well—trying to have someone sell the pastries at their store, websites, and even a food truck." I chuckle with how silly the last one sounds. "No takers, or it costs too much money. I can't keep it."

"Kaylan, sit down." I take a seat and he continues. "Your aunt only wanted you to try. She didn't want to make your life difficult or stress you out with this. I told you if in a few months things weren't good, you could look into selling it. It seems like it's time for that to happen. Thank you for giving it a chance. It means so much to me that you did. I know this made your life a bit crazy."

I look down at my feet, not wanting to look at him. "I just feel like I let everyone down. Also, what about Denise and Jessica? Now, they are going to be out of a job."

He places his hand on my shoulder. "Dear, don't worry about them. Denise was only doing this as a favor to your aunt. She doesn't need the job; she stayed on to try and help you. Sheryl asked her to before she passed away."

"And Jessica?" I look up into his eyes, and he gives me a small smile.

"She's young. She'll find another job. Don't worry about her."

The doorbell rings and Rob gets up to answer it. He returns with Dan in tow. I give him a small smile and we get down to business.

RETURNING BACK TO THE APARTMENT, I change out of my skirt and trudge down into the shop to see Jessica helping a customer. I give her a small smile and she returns the gesture. She knows things haven't gotten better, but she refrains from asking too many questions. Today, I'm going to have to tell them though, give them a heads up to begin looking for a replacement job. The customer gathers her items and leaves the shop, leaving just the three of us there.

"Hey, Denise, could you come out here for a minute?" I call back to her. "Jessica, can you have a seat?" I motion toward the table. Denise comes out from the kitchen and we all sit down at the small table, their eyes glued to mine. I take a deep breath and begin. "I am looking for a buyer for *The Sweet Shoppe*. Financially, things aren't good, and I haven't been able to turn things around. I've invested some of my own money into the place to keep it going, but sales just aren't where they used to be.

"I talked with the bank this morning to see about deferring the loan, or even refinancing, but it doesn't seem as though either of those are options for me. Ideally, I would like someone to come in and keep the shop going, but I don't think that's going to happen either. Dan told me a while ago, there was someone interested in the few shops around ours, in addition to ours, but Aunt Sheryl refused to sell it at that time. I've asked Dan to find a number for the person and see if they still want it. I know both of you must have questions."

"When are you closing the shop?" Jessica asks.

"We'll be able to keep the shop running for the next few weeks. I know this is going to be difficult for you both, having to locate another job, and I am so sorry about that. I truly am."

"Are you going back to the city then?" Denise asks.

"I'm not sure what I'm going to do. For right now, the shop is still running and I want to go out with a bang. We will continue operating like normal, and you are not to say anything to any of the customers, all right? We might get lucky and find a buyer who wants to keep the shop running. If not, then we will cross that bridge when we get there. This town is small enough that if any of us says something, word is bound to get around town."

They both nod in understanding as a customer walks in. Jessica puts on a smile and welcomes the customer while Denise and I head to the back.

"Dear, please don't feel bad about this. I know you tried your hardest. At least you can say that you are a much better baker after this experience," she says, trying to comfort me.

"Thanks, Denise, for everything. Uncle Rob told me you stayed on to help me out, and I appreciate it. You've taught me so much, and you have been wonderful to work with." I pick up a cookie and break off a piece before placing it in my mouth and chewing slowly. "Since we are going to be closing soon, I want to make a new recipe and sell that. Jack really enjoyed them when I made them for him, and I think others might as well.

"All right, what are you going to make?" she asks, her curiosity peaked.

I smile and begin pulling out the ingredients needed. "Brownies with chili peppers. It's sweet, and then on the back on your tongue, you get the kick of heat from the pepper."

"Those sound interesting. I guess there's no time like the present to try something new, right?" She smiles at me and carries the cookies out into the front of the shop.

Who knows? Maybe brownies are the key to saving this place.

CHAPTER NINETEEN

*T*he brownies are met with mixed reviews. Every day for the following week, I am outside passing out free samples to try to entice people into the shop. A few people couldn't wait to buy one, whereas others were not interested in the sweet heat. The samples did help drum up a little bit of business, but it still isn't going to be enough. I finish closing for the night and leave, locking the door behind me. I turn to find Jack is waiting for me.

"Hey, handsome, how was your day today?" I give him a quick kiss on the lips and unlock the door to the stairwell. We begin our walk upstairs to the apartment.

"It was fine. How was your day? Any chance there are some leftover brownies from today and you snagged me one?"

We walk into the apartment, and I hand him a bag with a brownie in it. He smiles wide and takes it quickly from me as if I was going to take it back. He takes a large bite and a small moan falls past his lips. "You know, I still love the éclairs, but these brownies might have become my new favorite thing on the menu. I am so happy my girlfriend knows how to bake."

"Well, I'm lucky I have a boyfriend who knows how to give me a workout; otherwise, I wouldn't be able to eat any of this stuff, and I've got to admit, I really did miss sugar. Now, give me a bite of that brownie," I say and watch as he pulls it away to protect it from me.

"I'll tell you what. You give me this recipe and I'll give you a bite?"

"No way, I'm taking the recipe to the grave with me." I get an idea and I smirk. I pull my shirt up over my head and watch his reaction. "I guess, since you won't share your treat with me, I won't share my treat with you. Enjoy that brownie. I'm going to take a shower by myself." I pull down my pants and kick them off, so I am standing there in just a bra and panties. His eyes are glued to my body, and I stretch, pretending I have no idea what I'm doing to him.

I walk toward the bathroom, and he comes up behind me, his fingers tracing the waistband of my panties. "If I give you a bite, will you let me join you in the shower?" His voice is low and husky.

I turn my head to the side and look at him over my shoulder. "I don't know, that depends on what you had in mind for the shower."

He presses his lips against my ear, and his fingers dance along the front of my panties. "You." He presses my panties up into me a little as he runs his fingers up and down my clit, a contented sigh passing my lips. I spread my legs a little more, allowing him room to work, and drop my head back onto his shoulder.

"How about we go to the bedroom instead? I'll let you have me however you want." I'm practically panting and my panties are soaked. He pushes me toward the bedroom and turns me around. Placing his hand on my chest, he pushes me down on the bed. I bounce up a bit and watch as he takes off his shirt. *I will never get tired of seeing abs like that!*

I unclasp my bra and pull it off my body, watching as he pulls his pants and boxers down his legs, his erect cock slapping his stomach. I bite the inside of my cheek to keep from moaning and watch as his eyes gloss over as he rakes over my body. "You're beautiful, Kaylan." He reaches out and grabs my ankle, pulling me toward the edge of the bed, and I let out a squeal of delight as he kneels down. He pulls my legs over his shoulders and brings his mouth to my core. He nudges my clit with his nose, and it's like an on-switch. I need him so bad.

"Please, Jack," I beg. "More, I need more." He drags my panties down my legs and attaches his mouth to my clit, his fingers sliding into my soaked core. I grab his hair and pull him closer, my hips thrusting up in time with his movements. He knows exactly what I like and shows no mercy when he is trying to make me come. "I'm so close, Jack," I pant. He swipes his thumb through my wetness and presses it against my tight hole. The extra sensation has me falling over the edge and my legs close around his head.

He holds me down and continues to lick me through my orgasm, and finally, I have to swat at him to make him stop. He stands and I pull myself further up the bed so my entire body is on it. He crashes his lips over mine, allowing me to taste myself on him. I buck my hips up, wanting to feel him sink himself in me. He places his arms on either side of my head, caging me, and the tip of his cock brushes against my swollen clit. I moan into the kiss.

Slowly, he presses in, not in a rush. The stretch feels so good, and I begin fluttering around him. "Not yet, baby. I want to take my time with you. I don't want this is too quick. I want to be able to savor every inch of you tonight." I nod my head, my eyes closed, enjoying every delicious sensation I'm feeling.

"Please move, Jack. Let me feel you." His thrusts are shallow and languid, and I can feel every bit of him as he moves. I rotate my hips to match his thrusts, my clit rubbing against his pelvis. I'm close again, and he flips us over so I'm riding him. I steady myself with my hands on his chest and start grinding down on him.

"Ride me, baby. I want to watch you come apart on me." He grabs hold of my hips, and I circle mine as he thrusts up. "I'm so close, baby. Fuck, you feel good." His thumb makes contact with my clit, and I hit my orgasm, shaking hard. He holds my hips and thrusts up a few more times before emptying in me. I collapse forward on him, both of us covered in a thin sheen of sweat and out of breath.

I smile and jump out to bed, running toward the kitchen. I hear Jack come out of the room, and I grab the brownie before he can get to it, taking a large bite from it. He laughs and tries to pull the rest away from me. "Finders keepers," I taunt. He wraps his arms around me and begins blowing raspberries on my neck, the vibrations making me laugh and shriek. "Okay, okay, you win." I hand the rest of the brownie back and he shoves it in his mouth, a victory smile on his lips.

CHAPTER TWENTY

My phone is buzzing and I look at the caller ID. It's Dan. I walk into the office and answer, closing the door gently behind me. "Hi, Dan. What's going on?"

"I have a few potential buyers that have reached out to me for the shop, and I wanted to run the information by you. Do you have a few minutes?"

"Yeah, can you let me get up into my apartment so I can have my laptop with me to take some notes?"

"Sure, call me back when you're available. I shouldn't take up too much of your time, but there are a few good offers here, and I think you would be wise to take one of them."

"Actually, would it be better to meet in person so you can go over the information with me?" I prop my elbows on the desk and place my head in my hand, a stress headache forming.

"Yeah, how about we meet at *Dark Roast* in thirty minutes? I'll buy you a coffee."

"All right, I won't turn down coffee. See you soon." I hang up the phone and open the office door to find Denise standing there listening in.

"Good news?" she asks, a small smile on her lips.

"Potential buyers, so if by good news you mean the bakery is saved, then probably not. I've got to meet with Dan. I'll let you know what he says, but he said I should consider one of these options because they are good. We will see what they are going to do with the place. I'll be back in a little bit. If you see Jack, tell him I'll be back soon. Do you want a coffee?"

"No, thank you though. I don't need more at this hour. I won't sleep tonight if I do." She laughs and goes back to rolling cake balls.

"Denise, it's only eleven in the morning!" I give her a look like she's insane.

"Yes, and I fall asleep on the couch most days by seven. Not all of us can be young and spend half the night awake."

I wave at her and chuckle as I shake my head. I step out into the front of the shop, and when Jessica is finished with a customer, I ask if she wants a cup of coffee. Her eyes light up at the prospect of caffeine and she gives me her order.

"All right, I should be back within an hour. I have a meeting with Dan."

She gives me a small smile. "Good luck."

"Thanks." I walk out the door and head toward my car, not wanting to be late.

The trip is quick, and Dan is already at a table in the back corner when I arrive. I take a seat opposite him and give him a pleasant smile. "Hey, Dan, thanks for the coffee." I take a sip and savor the flavor in my mouth. "All right, what do you have for me?"

"I just want to say how sorry I am again for this. I know I'm a big part of the blame for this, and I know this wasn't an easy choice for you."

"Dan, shit happens. My aunt's passing hit us all hard. I don't blame you. I'm kind of relieved in some form. Working two jobs has been difficult for the past few months, and it will be good to get some semblance of my life back." I still need to figure out everything with Jack, but I haven't wanted to talk to him about it yet because I didn't have information. "What are the offers you have?"

"Okay, this first one is offering to purchase the bakery, and they want everything including the recipes. They are offering a hefty sum, but they also want a clause in there that you won't sell them anywhere else."

I clasp my hands together and place them under my chin. "That seems a bit weird, and I don't know how I feel about giving up the recipes. I kind of like knowing those are staying within the family. What are they willing to offer?"

"They are willing to pay two-hundred and fifty thousand for it. It's a decent amount for the business, and it would be enough to pay off the rest of the loan and have some leftover." He hands me the sheet with the offer on it, so I can look over everything. I put it upside down, not wanting others to see the information, and wait for him to continue.

"All right, this offer is just for the building space, but it looks like they want to buy the two locations around you as well. They already have the other locations locked down with the landlord if you're willing to sell."

"What are they planning on doing with the spaces? Any idea?"

"I think they are going to put a restaurant in or something, so they are going to gut it and start over, knock down some walls and such."

"So *Little Sweet Shoppe* would officially be gone?" The small tremble in my voice doesn't go unnoticed.

His features soften as he looks at me. "If you take this offer, then yes. It looks like it."

I clear my throat. "How much are they willing to offer for it?"

"A hefty sum, they are extremely interested in buying. The buyer is willing to spend five-hundred thousand for it." He hands me the piece of paper, and I look at it and back at him, my eyes bugging out of my head.

"This can't be a serious offer, can it? Do you know who any of the buyers are?"

"It is a serious offer. I asked that question as well, and no, I don't know who the buyer is. Everything is going through their agent right now." I look at the paper again, still shocked by the sum of money they are willing to offer. Whoever wants it must really think the location is a prime spot for whatever restaurant that would go there. I flip the page over and look back at Dan.

"Thank you for handling all of this and working with the agent to get these offers. I appreciate it. I don't think I can to deal with this right now." I look over at the door as the small bell above it chimes. Jack walks in and locks eyes with me. He strides over to the table and sits down in the empty chair next to me.

"Hey, babe, I didn't know you were coming here. I was going to get a coffee to surprise you at the shop." He smiles and looks between Dan and me.

"Jack, this is Dan, my accountant," I begin the introductions. "Dan, this is Jack, my boyfriend."

"It's nice to meet you." Jack sticks his hand in Dan's outstretched one, a large smile on his face.

"You as well. Kaylan and I were just discussing—"

"How the bakery is doing better." I cut him off. "The brownies have been helping with sales a bit." I smile and give Dan a warning look to not say more.

"Oh, that's wonderful to hear, Kay. I'm happy for you guys. I know how much you want to be able to keep the shop going and all." He leans over and plants a small kiss on my cheek.

"Yeah, well, we need to finish business here, and then I

promised I'd bring Jessica back a coffee." I'm trying to get him to move on without being rude.

He puts his hands up in mock surrender. "Top secret business, I get it." He laughs. "I'll bring Jessica her coffee and meet you back at the shop. Can't wait for my brownie."

"You know, if you keep up with all the sugar, you're going to rot your teeth out or lose those perfect abs you worked so hard for." I smirk.

He smirks back. "Then stop making them and I'll stop buying them." He winks at me and gives me a quick kiss, making his way toward the counter for the coffees.

"Is there a reason you're not telling him?" Dan asks quietly.

"I don't know how to discuss me going back to the city for my real job yet, and up until today, I had no idea there were serious offers on the line." I look up at Jack as he takes the coffees from the barista and waves bye, walking out into the sunny street. "When do I have to give an answer by?"

"You have three days to make up your mind. Think hard about this one and let me know if you have questions. I can get answers from the agent quickly for you."

"After I choose, how long until the shop closes or is handed to the next owner?"

"About one month for each. It can be quicker if you choose the offer that will keep the shop operating.

I flip the pages over and look at the offers; one keeps *The Sweet Shoppe* open, the other closes it forever. One also is telling me I can't ever sell my aunt's recipes again, and the other is willing to pay a large amount to have the spot. I would be able to give some to Denise, Jessica, and my uncle and still have money to spare for myself. I begin thinking about the move back to the city. I would need an apartment and furniture. My gas bill is also going to be higher if Jack and I decide to do a long-distance relationship.

Jack. What am I going to tell him? He knows, if the shop doesn't start doing well, that I am going to have to sell it. I don't have the heart to tell him yet though. I'm falling so hard for this man. He seems almost perfect. He is there helping me through everything. Would it be so bad if I stayed here, found a new job maybe? It's not like my IT job is keeping me happy. I deal with pissy clients most of the day, and I am stuck in front of a computer all day.

Dan and I part ways, and I drive back to the shop. Jack waves at me from inside, and I motion to him that I will be back down soon. I take the papers upstairs and place them in a folder so I can review them later. I walk into the shop, and Jack is sitting there with his éclair and brownie in front of him.

"Wow, two things today, huh? Guess we are going to be running a bit longer than I thought."

"I wanted to have best of both worlds today." He smiles, and then his face turns serious. "Hey, I wanted to let you know Kevin has been contacting Oliver. He's still serious about opening a shop in the city. We are heading out there in an hour to meet with him."

"All right, why are you telling me this?"

"I didn't want you to hear it through the grapevine, and if Oliver thinks this the spot is good, we could be in business together. He wants to explore all options for opening another location, and he figured since Kevin is so persistent, why not look into it. I don't know if anything will come from it, but Oliver is insisting I go with him to check it out."

I place my petite hands over his large ones. "Are you planning on punching him again?"

He chuckles and shakes his head. "Unless the dick gives me a reason to, I don't think I will. I'll try to be on my best behavior." He makes an X over his heart with his index finger. "Scout's honor."

"Good, glad to hear it. I've got some work I need to get done tonight, so this actually works out well for me. I don't have to worry about you being a distraction."

"Baby, I'm a *wanted* distraction, and you can't say otherwise."

I smile at him. "Yes, you are. So, since you're leaving in an hour to *not* kick my ex's ass, I take it a run isn't happening today?"

"Oh, no, I'm sorry. Not today. You can always go by yourself though."

"Or I can take the day off, which sounds like a better idea to me. I'll just avoid all the sugar today. Any idea when you will be back?"

"Shouldn't be gone too long. If I make it back in time for dinner, do you want me to come by with food? Or we can always go to the diner or something."

"Yeah, sure. That sounds good to me. Keep me posted on how the day goes. It would be good if you guys open one in the city."

Cocking his head to the side, confused, he asks, "Why?"

I groan, not wanting to have this conversation right now, but know it's my fault for saying anything. "I might not be here much longer." I watch his face fall and see hundreds of questions flash across his eyes. "Listen, we can talk about it later. Now is not the time, and I'm sorry for saying anything at all. You have a meeting you have to get to, and I have work I have to get done. If we aren't too tired tonight, we can try to discuss it. If not, we will have to wait for the weekend. Okay?"

He pulls his hand out from under mine and crosses his muscular arms over his broad chest. "You said the shop was doing better when I saw you at the coffee shop."

"I did, and that is the truth. It is doing better, just not great. Can we please not do this right now?"

"Kaylan, how much do you need?"

I'm taken aback by his question and confused as to why he's asking. "Jack, I'm not taking your money."

"I want to help. How much?" he persists.

"Nothing, Jack. You can't help me with this one. I'm not letting you take the fall or using your money to help. That's what got you in trouble last time, taking the fall." The words slip past, and I cover my mouth, shock written on my features. I know how hard it was for him to tell me about Monica, and I all but threw it in his face that he is too caring for people. He pushes back his chair and stands quickly. "Fuck, Jack. I didn't mean it like that." I reach out for him and he pulls away.

"It's fine, Kaylan. I'm going to be late if I don't get out of here. We'll talk later." His voice is harsh and unforgiving. I sink down in my seat and my fingers reach for the hem of my shirt. A quiet, "Okay," manages to fall past my lips. He moves swiftly toward the door and leaves without another word.

"He's not too happy, huh?" Jessica asks, looking at me.

"No, I really think I messed that one up."

CHAPTER TWENTY-ONE

Me: *I'm sorry, Jack. That didn't come out how I meant it.*
Please call me when you are done in the city so we
can talk.

*I*t is the second text message I've sent him in the past few hours, and he hasn't responded to either of them. I'm hoping he isn't responding because he is just busy. I sit on the couch in the apartment and review the information Dan gave me. It is a big decision, and I don't want to make it alone. I dial Rob's number and wait patiently as it rings.

"Hello?" he answers.

"Hey, Uncle Rob, I wondered if I can come over and talk with you. Dan gave me a few options to go over, and I want to run everything by you as well, to get your thoughts."

"Sure, why don't you come by for dinner tonight? I'll make burgers on the grill. We can go over everything then. Is that all right?"

"Yeah, that sounds good. I appreciate it. Thanks, Uncle Rob."

"All right, dear, I'll see you tonight."

We disconnect the call, and I turn back to the papers to review. The first offer has the potential for more wiggle room on negotiations. I might be able to negotiate the recipes out of the deal for a slightly lower amount. That way, if I decide I want to try this again somewhere else, I can. I already have successful recipes under my belt, so it would just be a matter of getting a loan and a location to start up the business.

On the other hand, the amount of money the second offer is willing to give would be enough to start a bakery somewhere else. It breaks my heart knowing the bakery would have to close permanently though. The bakery has been around for as long as I can remember, and to lose it feels like I would be losing another part of my life that I'm not sure I want to let go.

My phone lights up with an incoming message. My heart races, hoping it's Jack. I look at the ID and see it is from Kevin. *What the fuck does he want?* I take a deep breath and open it.

Kevin: *Met with your boyfriend and Oliver today. I wanted to apologize for how I acted the last time we saw one another. What I did wasn't right. I was jealous. They both seem like good guys, and I hope we are able to work together. Oliver seemed excited about the location I was showing them.*

What the hell? I'm so taken aback by the text that I read it two more times to make sure I understand correctly. I type and delete a reply a few times before finally settling on something simple.

Me: *Thank you.*

I'm not telling him that I forgive him, because I definitely don't forgive him for how he acted or what he said, but I'm not ignoring him either.

If I'm getting this text, that means they are done and probably heading back now. I decide to send one more message to Jack, hoping he will answer.

Me: *I'm having dinner at my uncle's tonight.*

I sit there, staring at my phone, willing him to respond. Finally giving up after a few minutes, I gather my stuff and make my way over to my uncle's, hoping we'll talk in the morning.

WE SIT in his living room, reviewing the information Dan gave me as we nibble on some cookies I brought from the bakery. Rob's ankle rests comfortably on his knee, and he's relaxed back into the couch as he reads over both offers. I sit next to him quietly, waiting for him to say something and give me advice.

"Whatever I end up choosing, I want you to know I plan on giving you some of the money. This was Sheryl's store, and it's only fair that you get some of it, too."

He puts the paper down and pulls his reading glass down his nose to look at me over the top of them. "Kaylan, your aunt and I have our ducks in a row. Financially, I'm set. You aren't giving me any of the money from this sale. Sheryl would have my head, and I know she's watching me. Now, I've reviewed both offers. Which one are you leaning toward?"

"I don't know. I mean, this first offer keeps the shop going, even if I'm not the one running it, but I don't like that I'd have to give up the rights to the recipes. I keep thinking maybe I would have some pull, however. I could accept their offer for a lower amount with the stipulation that I get to keep the recipes."

He rocks his head from side to side, weighing the options. "So, what happens when they want to change the name and the decor and make it their own shop? The offer states they want to keep the shop running, but it doesn't mention anything about them keeping it the same. I think this one is basically a way to get the recipes from you." He laughs quietly. "People always were trying to buy those damn recipes from your aunt. Did you know she hosted an event in the shop once where people had to try to replicate her treats?"

I smile at him and shake my head. "No, she never told me about that. Do you have pictures? What was the prize?"

"I know there are pictures somewhere, but I don't know where exactly. There was a huge tasting, and people from town got to try the different creations. The prize, though, was a copy of the recipe for her oatmeal raisin cookies. You would have thought someone was winning the lottery with the way people scrambled for it." I watch the distant look in his eyes as he travels down memory lane.

I feel wrapped up in his memory with him. "Who won, do you remember?"

He shakes his head. "I don't, but whoever it was, I bet they still couldn't make the cookies as good as she could. She had a real knack for it. The only person that has come close, besides Denise, is you. You're good at baking, Kaylan, and you picked it up so quickly. I'm so proud of everything you've done, and I appreciate that you gave it a go." He reaches forward and places a reassuring hand on my knee, giving it a gentle squeeze. "Now, if you want my honest opinion between these two options, I would say it's time to let it go and move on. Go with the second option."

I nod my head. That is the way I am leaning as well, and to hear him confirm it is a weight off my shoulders. He's giving me permission to let go of the shop. "Honestly, that's the offer I was leaning toward as well, but I was nervous about your thoughts of closing for good."

"It's for the best. Take the offer, Kaylan, and move on."

JACK STILL HASN'T RETURNED any of my messages, and I am getting worried that something happened to him. I decide, since he lives close to my uncle's house, that I'll run by and see if he is home. I pull into the driveway, but the house is dark and his Jeep isn't here. I feel sick knowing he isn't back here. *Calm down, he's probably at my place then.*

I turn the car around and go home as fast as I can. I breathe a sigh of relief when I see his Jeep in the parking lot. I pull in next to him, and we both get out of our cars. He walks up to me and extends his hand, a long-stemmed rose nestled between his fingers.

"Sorry I haven't responded to you today. It's been," he pauses, searching for the right word, "interesting. I know you didn't mean what you said, and I'm sorry I took it like that. Monica is a sensitive subject, and I don't tell many people about her. I don't want the judgment. My nerves were already a bit fried because I was going to see Kevin again, and I didn't want to."

I place my fingers over his lips to quiet him. "No, Jack, I'm sorry. As soon as I said it, I wanted to take it back. We have a lot to talk about though. Let's go upstairs and talk."

CHAPTER TWENTY-TWO

*W*ord spreads quickly that the shop is closing, and just like any other thing that is going away, people want it. It has been a mad rush over the past three weeks. There are constant lines throughout certain points of the day, and we are having a difficult time keeping up with demand on the weekends. Our doors close permanently at the end of the day today. I arranged to head back to work in two weeks with Karen, telling her I need a break from the constant work first. I also need to find an apartment. Jack was upset when I explained everything, but we are going to find a way to make it work.

I work in tandem with Jessica as we ring up our last customers of the night, getting ready to close up. The signing of all the papers is tomorrow, and I want to be able to get anything out that we want. I open a bottle of champagne, trying to keep this as happy as possible.

"Ladies, it has been wonderful getting to know the both of you. Thank you for everything you have done to help me and this place." I pour the drinks into some flutes and hand one to each of them. I hold mine up in a toast. "To future happiness, and a bit of sugar."

"To a bit of sugar," they chime in, and we all take a sip.

"Jessica, what are you going to do now that the shop is closing?" I ask, picking up a leftover cookie and taking a bite.

"School starts in a week, so I will be leaving to go back to college, but Jack offered me a job as a hostess at *Red Bird* when I'm home for holidays and such. So, I'll be all right." She shrugs and takes a sip of champagne.

"I'm glad to hear you got something else." I turn my attention to Denise. "And you? Planning on actually retiring and enjoying life?"

"I am planning on taking a nice vacation and relaxing with my husband. Maybe we will book a cruise. I don't know. When are you heading back to the city?"

"I have to sign the papers tomorrow, but I worked it out in the deal that I can stay in the apartment for another week, so that gives me time to get an apartment in the city and get my stuff back up there." My eyes water, and I bite my lip to keep it from trembling. "I'm going to miss it here though. I've gotten so used to the small town feel of everything, and I'm not sure I really want to go back."

"Why don't you stay then? I'm sure your hunky boyfriend wouldn't mind if you moved in with him. You've told me before you don't care for your job, so why not find a new one?"

I rub my forehead and squint. "It's not that easy. I have a whole life and some loose ends I have to take care of. Jack and I have talked about it, and while neither of us wants this to happen, he understands why I have to head back. We'll figure it out."

We sit at a table talking and drinking until the bottle is empty. Each of us picks up a chair and places it upside down on the table. As we leave the empty bakery, I begin to cry. This is it; it's really over. I just keep hoping that whoever bought the shop keeps the memory alive somehow. Maybe they will keep a small piece of the sign and hang it up, or maybe try to make one of the desserts. I lock the door and see Jack waiting outside for me with a few brown paper bags.

"I got Chinese for dinner. Thought we could cuddle and watch a movie or something. I can't stay the night, but I wanted to see you tonight, make sure you are doing okay."

"I am, thanks. We've had the best business these last few weeks than we had in months. Too bad these people didn't get their butts in gear sooner. It would have saved me a lot of time and heartache. It's for the best though, and we'll be all right. The city isn't that far away, and I'm sure we can find a way to make things work. You never did tell me about the location in the city. I know Oliver was going back and forth. Did you guys decide to move forward?"

"No, we both decided now isn't the right time."

The evening is quiet, and after watching some movie neither one of us is paying attention to, Jack leaves for the evening.

"You let me know as soon as it's over, and if I'm out of my meeting, I'll meet you so we can go apartment hunting for you. I want to make sure you're somewhere safe, since I can't convince you to stay here with me. By the way," he waits until I'm looking into his blue eyes, "are you sure I can't convince you to stay? I make a mean bowl of cereal in the morning," he teases.

"Ah, the infamous meal that I have yet to receive from you." I play along with him. "Not right now. I need to figure out what I'm going to do, but in the meantime, I have to be able to pay my bills. Student loans aren't going to pay for themselves." I place my hands against his chest and capture his lips with mine. He wraps his arms around me and holds me close as he deepens the kiss, my mouth opening to his. I pull back first, and he leans forward, trying to bring me back to him. "Goodnight, Jack."

"Night, Kay. I love you, baby."

"I love you, too."

I SIT in the attorney's office, my knees bouncing a mile a minute and my palm keeps gathering a fine sheen of sweat due to nerves. Uncle Rob and Dan both offered to come with me today, but I told them no. I have to do this alone. *Deep breaths.* I stand and grab a glass of water from the water cooler and sit back down, waiting for the buyers to arrive.

"I'm so sorry about this. I'm not sure why they are so late. They should be here any minute."

"It's all right. Actually, where is the restroom?"

"Down the hall to your left. Just come back here once you're set and hopefully we can get started."

I walk down the hall, following the instructions she provides, and lock the door behind me. Walking to the sink, I place my hands on either side of it and stare at my reflection. I applied a subtle amount of make-up to my face this morning, just enough to frame my honey brown eyes. I have my hair pulled back into a side chignon, and I'm wearing a navy polka dot shirt dress with a tie around my waist. For shoes, I settled on a pair of ballet flats— business casual, yet comfortable.

I grab a few paper towels from the holder and run them under the cold water. After wringing them out, I blot my face and neck, trying to help with my nerves. When I am as calm as possible, I walk back toward the room. I hear a few voices talking and pick up on one of them being male. Taking a breath in through my nose and pushing it out through my mouth, I put a smile on my face and enter the room, three sets of eyes landing on me.

I scan their faces, and as soon as my eyes land on him, I feel my entire world crumble around me.

"Jack?"

CHAPTER TWENTY-THREE

*H*e pushes his chair back and stands up quickly. "What are you doing here?"

"I think the better questions is what are you doing here?" I ask, still in shock.

"I'm here for the sign—" He stops himself and looks at Olivier. "Fuck."

My heartbeat is so loud it's drumming in my ears. I can't do this. I can't deal with the man I love closing the place I love because he wants to make money. I look over at my attorney, who is watching our conversation like a ping pong match. I harden my facial features and emotions, and I say, "I give you power of attorney. Sign everything." Turning on my heel, I practically run out of the office and to the elevator. I press the down button a least a dozen times, and when I hear Jack's voice, I opt for the stairs.

He knew I was going to be going down, so I decide to go up a floor to throw him off. I run up a flight of stairs and press my back against the wall so he can't see me.

"Kaylan," I hear him yell as he descends the stairs toward the bottom floor. I hold my breath, not wanting to give away my location. My phone starts ringing, and I pull it out of my purse quickly to silence it. Jack. I knew he would call; I just didn't think it would be this soon. I ignore the call and turn it off. I can't talk to him right now. After hanging out in the dingy stairwell for another few minutes, I risk exiting the building, figuring he returned to sign the papers.

I look around the hallway. Upon seeing no one, I dart out to my car and lock the door as soon as I sit down. My tears sting my eyes and my throat burns from holding back as long as I have. *Hold it together until you get home.* I clear my throat and drive home as fast as I can. I know Jack is going to come looking for me as soon as he's done stomping on my heart.

I run up into the apartment, gather a few personal items, and head back down to my car, saying a silent prayer with each step I take. *Please don't let him be done.* I don't see him, so I get into my car and race to my uncle's house. I know he won't have a problem with me crashing there.

I pull into his driveway and break down. The tears fall from my eyes in heavy droplets, staining my dress. *I can't believe I thought he loved me.* I allow myself a few minutes to feel bad for myself, and then I get mad. *He knew how much trouble the bakery was in, and he agreed to this anyway.* Jack knew what the bakery meant to me, and how much I was doing to try to keep it going, and he swooped in and stole it from me.

I wipe my eyes and grab my overnight bag, then head up to my uncle's front door and ring the doorbell. He opens the door and looks at me, his features softening as he looks into my eyes. "All done with the signing?"

"I don't know. I told my attorney she could sign everything and got out of there."

"Was it too much? See the new owners and all?" he asks, moving out of the way so I can walk in.

"Yeah, something like that. I would prefer not to talk about it right now. Would you mind if I crashed here for the night? I don't want to stay in my apartment." I set my bag down and turn to look toward him, not meeting his eyes.

"Are you having a fight with that boy, Jack?"

"Something like that." I continue to look around the room and watch him nod his head. "Great, let me go put my bag down and then maybe I can whip something up for us? Are you hungry?"

"Not really, do you want a beer or something? Looks like it was a rough morning for you."

"Yeah, I really would. Thanks."

I walk upstairs and drop my stuff off in the spare bedroom at the beginning of the hallway. I take a quick peek at myself in the mirror and realize I look like hell. Grabbing a tissue from my purse, I wipe some of my smudged mascara from under my eyes. I shrug at my reflection. I'm probably not going to look much better than this.

I change into some yoga pants and a t-shirt, tossing my dress into my bag. I know I can't run away forever, but I need more time to get my head on straight before I talk with him. Walking downstairs, I take the beer out of Rob's outstretched hand, and the two of us head to the back of the house to sit outside.

"Do you want to talk about it?"

"He was there, Uncle Rob. He was the person buying the shop, right out from underneath me. He knew how much it killed me to have to close this place, and he swooped in to open another restaurant. I'm starting to wonder if he planned this once he heard the place was closing. When I first met him, he said Oliver was looking at a place in town to do it but the owner didn't want to sell." My eyes widen, and my lips part as a lightbulb goes off. "Son of a bitch, *The Sweet Shoppe* was the shop that didn't want to sell."

"Are you sure? It could have been another location," he tries reasoning.

"No. Why else would the price he was offering be so high if it wasn't to make sure I would jump?" I'm angry now. My blood is boiling and I am seeing red. I take a few deep breaths to try and calm my nerves. *Jack Madison can rot in hell!* "Uncle Rob, I can't go back to that apartment. I can't see Jack. I'm going to leave to go back to the city tomorrow morning. Would you be willing to clean out the apartment, and I can come in a few weeks to get everything from you?" I see the look of hesitation and I continue. "You know, never mind. I'll hire a company to get it all out and bring it to me."

"I don't mind, Kaylan. I can do it. I just feel you're making a rash decision. Give him a chance to explain. Maybe there is a good reason."

"No, I'm going to get the moving company. I'm going to make a few calls to see when they'll be able to get everything out, and I need to call some friends to see where I can crash until I can get into an apartment of my own."

I give him a kiss on the cheek and go back upstairs into the bedroom to retrieve my phone. I hit the power button and wait for it to hum to life. My heart is beating like crazy, the anticipation killing me. It finishes powering up and I have thirty-two unread texts and five voicemails. All but two of the texts are from Jack.

I close out of the messages from Jack, not caring about what he wants, and look at the one from Denise.

Denise: *Hey, how did the close go? Your aunt would have been proud of you. Just remember that.*

I type a quick reply.

Me: *It's over. That's all that matters.*

Next, I open the other text from my friend Katie.

Katie: *When are you coming back? We need to get drinks soon so you can tell me all about what's happened since I saw you last!*

Me: *I'm coming back tomorrow. Can I crash on your couch until I find a place and have my stuff from here delivered there? I'm hoping it only takes a few days.*

Her reply seems to take forever and finally my phone chirps with a reply.

Katie: *Of course! Anything you need, you know that.*

I reply with a quick thanks and let her know I'll give her details a little later. I dial into my voicemail and begin listening. The first one is from Jack, and I skip it without even listening to a word he says.

The next one is from the attorney. "Hello, Ms. Santine. I'm calling to let you know the signing is complete, and I will mail you a copy for your records. Please call me back with an address I can send it to. Thank you."

I will call her back in a little while and also apologize for my behavior. The next one is from Jack. "Kaylan, please call me. I need to tell you what's going on—" I hit delete, not wanting to hear the rest of it. The last two are also from him, each one sounding more defeated than the last one. Another call comes in from him, and I let it ring until it goes to voicemail. My heart is breaking all over, and a sob breaks through.

My phone chimes with a new voicemail and I call into it.

Why am I torturing myself with this? I type in my passcode, and Jack's husky voice filters through to my ear. "Please call me, Kaylan. I don't know where you are, and I'm worried sick. At least let me know you are all right. I want the chance to explain, but for now, I'll settle for your safety." The voicemail ends with a low click, and I end the call with it. He sounds so defeated and worried.

I open the texts from him and type a new one, not wanting to see the others he sent.

Me: *I'm fine. Leave me alone and stop calling.*

Within seconds, I begin receiving texts one right after another.

Jack: *Where are you?*
Jack: *We need to talk. Please let me explain.*
Jack: *I didn't know.*
Jack: *Kaylan, please tell me where you are so I can come and talk to you.*

I ignore all of his messages and contemplate blocking his number entirely, but can't get myself to do it. I begin my search for a moving company and find one that is able to come in tomorrow and get everything packed and out to me in the city. Perfect. I give them a meeting place to get the keys from me and go back downstairs to see Uncle Rob.

"Kaylan, I'm going to go to the store. Do you want me to get you anything?"

"No, I'm okay, thanks." I sit on the couch and take a long sip of my beer, now warm from sitting. I really want to go out for a run to burn off some pent-up energy, but Jack lives close to my uncle's house and I don't want to risk him finding me. I hear Rob leave and sit alone, ignoring all the messages and phone calls that keep coming in. *When is he going to get the hint?*

I can't stand it anymore and I finally answer one of his calls. "I don't want to hear whatever it is you want to tell me. I'm leaving for the city tomorrow. Stop. Calling. Me." I enunciate all my words and try to hang up.

"Please wait, Kaylan. Don't hang up. Just let me talk to you." I don't respond, but I don't hang up either. I can hear him breathing through the line. "Kay? Are you still there?"

"You have thirty seconds."

"I didn't know the place we were buying included *The Sweet Shoppe*. I knew Oliver was looking in that area, and with the foot traffic and the amount of business in the area, we would be fools to not want to move to that location."

"Good luck with everything, Jack. If you keep calling, I'm blocking your number." I hang up the phone and pull myself together. The small voice in the back of my head is yelling at me though. *Let him explain. What does he have to hide from you?* I'm not in the right frame of mind to talk to him though, not yet anyway.

CHAPTER TWENTY-FOUR

*T*he calls stop for the day, as do the texts, with the exception of one at night.

Jack: *Good night, beautiful. I hope you allow me to talk to you soon. Please don't block me.*

I don't respond. My silent tears stream down my face until I finally pass out from emotional exhaustion. My dreams are filled with images of Jack, and I wake up with enough heartache I think I might explode. I clutch my chest and take a few deep, calming breaths. In... Out... In... Out. The clock on the nightstand says it's two o'clock, and I figure Jack will be home sleeping.

I tiptoe down the stairs, gather my keys and purse, hop in my car, and drive back toward my apartment. The roads are empty and the night is cool. I roll down my windows and take a deep breath of the fresh air, hoping to clear my thoughts. When I turn onto my street and see my apartment building up ahead, my heart sinks. His Jeep is parked on the side of the road.

I was hoping I could go inside and get more of my stuff so the movers didn't have as much to do, but I'm too afraid to getting out of the car because I don't want to see him. I turn off my headlights and pull into a spot a few spaces over from him. I peer toward his Jeep and see his form leaning against the back of his seat, his eyes closed and his mouth slightly parted. *He's sleeping here waiting for me.* A sad smile creeps across my face at the thought.

After returning to Uncle Rob's house, I leave him a note stating I'm going to get an early start to the city. He doesn't need to know what time I left, and I feel like the faster I can get away, the better. I know it will be a few hours until Katie will answer any message I send, so I go to the diner for a quick, quiet breakfast. Walking in, I spot Steph, and she smiles at me.

"Hey, hun, how's everything going? I haven't seen you in a few weeks." She looks past me and then locks eyes with me again. "Just you this morning?"

"Yeah, Steph, just me." She nods and gives me a small smile. I can tell she is itching to ask questions, but thankfully, she remains silent. I follow her to a small booth and ask for a cup of coffee. I'm not hungry, but I know I should try to eat something, so I order an omelet with a side of fruit and bacon. My screen lights up and I see I have another message from Jack; he must have woken up. My heart constricts thinking of him sleeping there instead of his comfortable bed.

Jack: *Good morning, beautiful. I hope you slept well. Whenever you are willing to talk to me, I'll be here. Please don't block me.*

I look at it, smile, and put my phone back down. Breakfast is quiet until Steph can't contain it anymore. She sits in the booth across from me and waits. We have a small stare down until I finally speak first. "Good morning, Steph. Can I help you?"

"Where's Jack?"

"Last time I saw him, he was buying my bakery out from under me without my knowledge." *Okay, it was a lie. He was sleeping soundly in his car outside my apartment.*

"That doesn't sound like something Jack would do. Are you sure? Maybe you just need to give him a chance to explain."

I cradle my cheek in my palm and look at her. "You called him, didn't you?"

"Please just listen to him? He called earlier and told me if I saw you to let him know." I watch as she looks past me, toward the front door. He's here. I can feel his presence and my spine stiffens. I watch as she slides out of the booth and makes her way toward him. I want to turn and see him, to look into his caring blue eyes, but I can't bring myself to. I know he's walking closer toward me and can smell him as he steps into my space.

I clench my hand into a fist and try to keep the hurt out of my voice for the conversation I know is about to happen.

"Hey, Kay," he says, sounding broken. He takes a seat and combs his fingers through his hair. "We need to talk. You need to understand I had no idea your shop was part of what we were purchasing."

I glare at him but manage to keep my voice low. "I don't see how it's possible that your business partner was able to pull one over on you. You mean to tell me that, when he told you the location he wanted to buy, you didn't stop and say 'hmm, that is the same building as Kaylan's shop'. Maybe I should give her a heads up'?"

"I didn't know you were selling it right away. We never discussed it." His voice is rising in anger. He has *no right* to get angry. He is the one who bought my shop out from under me.

I take a deep breath, close my eyes, and count to five. When I open them, he's watching me intently. "Well, now it's sold and nothing can change that." I pull enough money out of my wallet to cover my barely eaten breakfast, coffee, and a generous tip and stand up. He mirrors my movements, towering over me as he stands. "I'm heading back to the city today, and the movers will be by to collect my things later today. Good luck with the restaurant. I wish you and Oliver all the success in the world."

"Kaylan, please don't leave like this. You haven't given me the chance to explain anything." He takes a step toward me and places a gentle hand on my cheek. I nuzzle into it momentarily and turn my face so I can kiss his palm. I wrap my arms around myself and turn away from him, walking out of the diner and to my car. I glance back and see him standing there, defeated. His head is hanging low, and Steph is by his side. I start crying all over again.

CHAPTER TWENTY-FIVE

*T*arrive at Katie's a little after eight in the morning. I had to stop a few times and have a good cry. She ushers me into her apartment and I collapse on the couch, tucking my legs up under me.

"Spill. What happened? Why were you in such a rush to get out of there?"

"So, you know I went down to run my aunt's shop after she passed away, right?" We talked about it a few weeks ago over drinks. I know she remembers.

"Yes, I also know you told me you were going to send me homemade goodies, but that never happened," she teases.

"Well, you could have come down and gotten them, too, you know." I sass back, a smile breaking out on my face. "Anyway, I had to sell the shop. We weren't able to make ends meet, and I decided to sell it to someone that wanted to turn the shop and the open spots around it into a restaurant. It's a great spot so it makes sense."

"Okay, I'm failing to see the problem in this. You had to sell, and you knew whoever bought wouldn't keep it a bakery."

"Right. The problem is the guy I started dating, Jack, bought it out from under me and didn't tell me until I saw him at the signing."

Her mouth forms a giant O shape and she nods, understanding. "Have you talked to him about it? Does he know what he did was stupid?"

Why is it that she sounds like everyone else? "He told me he didn't know the location included my shop. I don't see how that's possible at all."

"So, let me ask you. Are you upset because he's the one who bought the shop and is going to close it? Or are you upset because he didn't tell you he was buying it?"

I think about it before answering. "I guess a bit of both. He knew I was going to have to sell the shop and everything, but I feel so betrayed that it's *him*. I had a feeling going into this that the shop was going to close, but it would be so much easier if I didn't know the person buying it. I could have just signed the papers and moved on." I push out a deep breath, trying to keep my emotions in check.

"Kaylan, do you like this guy? Is he better than Kevin?"

Without missing a beat, I respond, "Yes, Katie. I love him. I don't know if I can trust him after this though. It's a lot to handle. He texted and called all night, and I left him standing alone in a diner this morning to come here. He looked like he'd just lost the world."

"Why don't you text him, or call him, and let him know that? He's probably heartbroken just like you." She places her hand on my forearm and gives it a gentle squeeze. "I'm going to get some coffee. Do you want a cup?" I nod, and she walks toward the kitchen, leaving me alone to make the choice.

Opening my phone, I pull up Jack's name and send him a text.

Me: *Just give me some time.*

His response comes seconds later.

Jack: *Let me know when you're ready. I'll be here waiting. I love you.*

I lock my phone and look at Katie as she brings the coffee to me. "So, when are we finding you an apartment? I promise you can stay as long as you need, but I need to know if you are going to be out sooner than later." She winks at me and takes a sip of hers.

I GET SETTLED in my new apartment and am back into the groove of things. I stayed with Katie for only about two weeks before I was able to get into my new one-bedroom space. It isn't big, but it suits my needs just fine. Uncle Rob allowed me to take everything that was in the apartment upstairs from the bakery, so I didn't have to worry about furnishing this place. That was taken care of.

Karen is happy to have me back at work, as are my co-workers. While I'm happy to be back in the swing of things, it doesn't feel right. I am missing something important and I know what it is. I'm missing Jack and the bakery. This job, this life isn't what I want any more. I want to live in a small town with my handsome boyfriend, where I can wake up tangled in his limbs every morning. I want to have flour on my cheeks and in my hair and smell like sugar and chocolate.

It's been nearly a month since I last contacted Jack. He hasn't tried to contact me since our conversation the day I left. I've written and deleted so many texts to him; I'm just not sure where to start or how to say what I need to say. I unlock my phone and pull up the messages. I type three simple words:

Me: *Can we talk?*

As if he knew I was going to text him, he responds immediately with one word.

Jack: *When?*

Me: *Tonight at 7? We can meet somewhere in between if that's okay with you.*

Jack: *I'll come to you. Tell me where and I'll be there.*

Me: *The Blue Lagoon. Do you know where it is?*

Jack: *I'll find it. Thank you, Kaylan.*

I stare at his words as another text comes in from him.

Jack: *I love you.*

I feel the weight of the world roll off my shoulders by looking at those three simple words. He loves me. He *still* loves me. I don't want to get my hopes up for the night, but I will listen to everything he has to say.

At a quarter to seven, and I am sitting at the bar, slowly sipping on a glass of Shiraz. My stomach feels like it's in knots, and I keep looking around. *I'm here early. Don't worry, he will show.* He walks through the front glass door and I want to melt into a puddle. He is more beautiful than I remember him being. As he nears me, though, I notice he has bags under his eyes, and his shoulders are drooping. He sits next to me and his scent clouds my senses. I want to reach out and touch him, but I pull my hand back at the last second. His eyes hold mine and I sit frozen, staring at his beautiful face.

"Hey, Jack. How ya been?" I ask, keeping my voice down.

He gives a small chuckle and shakes his head. "Better now that I'm looking at you. I've missed you so much, Kaylan. Thank you for giving me the chance to talk to you."

"Do you want something to drink?" I motion toward the bar.

He shakes his head. "I've been doing that a little too much lately. It's better if I don't." His admission breaks my heart, and I reach my hand out and place it on his arm that's resting on the bar. I feel the familiar warmth in the pit of my stomach and pull my hand back instantly. When I finally get the courage to look into his eyes, they are hooded and lust-filled. I imagine I look the same and I bite my lip. "Please don't do that," he whispers just loud enough for me to hear.

I pull my lip out of my teeth and speak. "Explain. What happened?"

He looks at me silently as he tries to focus on his words. "Oliver told me back when I first met you that there was a place he was seriously considering in town because of the great location. He didn't give me many details except for the fact that the owner wouldn't sell. I didn't think much else on it and forgot about it. Flash forward to when the offer was given. Oliver told me the location, and I thought it would be great because then I would be able to see you more. It was going to be next to the shop. You happened to tell me that same night that you were selling the place. I called up the agent and told her to put in an offer on *just* your bakery."

"What do you mean?"

"You had several offers on your shop, right?" I nod my head and take a small sip of wine, trying to stop the fluttering in my stomach. "I was one of those offers. You didn't accept mine, though, and I was heartbroken. I didn't want to tell you I put one in because I didn't want you to think I was trying to go behind your back."

I feel a lump form in my throat and speak past it. "What was your offer? Dan didn't tell me all of them, just two that were real contenders."

"I offered a quarter of a million for it and possession of the recipes."

I think I'm going to be sick!

CHAPTER TWENTY-SIX

*I*t's a good thing I'm sitting. I think I might pass out if I wasn't. "What? Why?"

"I didn't want you to move back into the city and start your own bakery. I was trying to find a way to get you to stay. If you had accepted the offer, I was going to tell you that night. We would have been co-owners." I feel as though I'm underwater; I hear his words, but everything seems muffled. "Kaylan, please say something."

"I didn't want to give up my recipes because they were my aunt's, not because I wanted to open a new shop with them. That's the reason I didn't go with that offer. I knew the bakery would have stayed open, but I didn't like the fact the recipes wouldn't be mine anymore. I also didn't like the unknown factor in all of it."

He shoves his hands through his hair. "Fuck. I really messed this one up. Kaylan, I am so sorry. Please believe me. Until you walked through the door that day, I had no idea we were purchasing your shop, too. I figured you must have gone with another offer, and I didn't want to pry because it was none of my business. I thought we were only buying the shops next to you, and I was planning on telling you after the signing. I knew you were going to have a rough day as you were signing the bakery away, so Oliver was going to make us a nice dinner. My plans for the night included cuddling around you to make you feel better and lots of treats."

I feel like such an idiot. I should have told him everything and brought him into the discussion as well. While he had no say in the business, it would have been nice to get his opinion. "I'm so sorry, Jack."

"Please come home, baby. I miss you so much. I haven't been able to function well since you left." He grabs my hand and holds it between his large ones. He rubs small circles on the back of my hand, and goosebumps rise in their wake.

"Jack, I can't just leave. I have work here and an apartment I just moved into." It's the truth, but it sounds like an excuse, even to my ears. I watch his face fall, and I'm breaking with him all over again.

"I understand. Can I come to visit at least? I can take you on some dates. We can try this again, slowly, if that's what you want. I'll tell you everything this time. No secrets." He is all but begging. What he is asking is everything I want, too. I miss him just as much as he misses me.

I smile at him. "I'd like that. We can try."

His smile lights up his entire face. He takes my hand in his and lifts it to his lips to kiss the back of it. His lips are a bit rough, he probably hasn't been drinking enough water, but it still shoots heat to my core. I fidget in my seat, and he notices. He pulls me closer to him and brushes his lips against my ear. "Good to know I still turn you on."

I let out a tiny, shaky breath and pull back to look into his eyes. "It would be hard to not get turned on. Have you seen what you look like?"

He laughs. "Not as beautiful as you are." He runs the back of his finger along my jaw. I flutter my eyes closed and lean into his touch. Opening my eyes, I cover his hand with mine and hold him in place.

"Do you want to come over? We can talk a bit more. I have a few questions I still want answered, and we might be more comfortable there."

"Only if that's what you really want. I'm not going to push anything with you."

"It's what I want. Please?"

"All right."

He pays my tab for the glass of wine I barely touched, and we head to my apartment on the other side of town. I keep glancing in my rearview mirror, making sure I don't lose him in the traffic. We pull into the parking lot, and he parks his Jeep next to my car. Walking toward the building, our hands brush against one another's. When he takes mine and intertwines our fingers, I look down at our hands and back up at him. He looks much happier than when he first arrived at the bar tonight. More relaxed.

The electric current that's running through our fingers is making me dizzy, and I'm happy when I have a moment of reprieve to fish my keys out of my purse to open the apartment door. He follows me inside and closes the door behind him.

"Can I get you anything to drink?" I wrap my arms around myself, suddenly nervous with him in my apartment. It isn't a big space, and his frame seems to dominate a large portion of the room. He shakes his head, takes a seat, and pats the seat next to him.

"Why don't you just ask me what you want to ask?"

I take a seat and gather my thoughts. "You've told me my aunt helped you get back on track by giving you odd jobs and such, but there are a few things I'm still not sure about." I pause to gauge his reaction before continuing. "When my aunt was helping you, where did you stay?"

He smiles as if he knew this was coming. "The apartment above the shop. I didn't have much to my name, as most of it got thrown out after the whole issue with Monica. Since rent at my apartment wasn't getting paid, the complex had someone clean my stuff out. Your aunt bought me a few clothes that I could wear." He chuckles. "The clothes you found are actually mine."

"Why didn't you tell me?"

"I thought it would be weird. Hey, Kaylan, I used to live here for a short time while I was getting back on my feet. I used to dream about the girl eating batter out of a bowl from a picture I saw."

I look at him, shocked. He leans closer to me, his eyes burning into mine.

"I've wanted to meet you since I first laid eyes on that picture of you. I began asking your aunt all sorts of questions about you, and she gave me updates whenever she saw me once I stopped working for her. After she passed away and I saw you in the bedroom, I thought it was a dream." He jabs his fingers through his hair. "You're my perfect girl, and I was selfish and needy. I never used to go to the shop for an éclair every day. I started showing up hoping to see you."

"Really?" Tears are beginning to form, and I turn my head away from him. I don't want him to see me cry again.

He places his index finger and thumb on my chin and turns my gaze back to him. "Really. Let me tell you, it wasn't easy trying to control myself around you, knowing you were with someone else. Imagine my luck when he turned out to be a bastard."

The smug look on his face has me stifling a giggle.

"Do you want to spend the night?"

His eyes light up at the prospect, but he shakes his head. "I don't want to rush anything tonight, so maybe soon, but tonight isn't a good idea." I understand and agree, but that doesn't make it any less sad. "Would you be willing to come down next week? I have something I want to show you."

"Can you tell me what it is?"

"No, you need to see it yourself. I think you may like it."

"Any hints?"

"No, just promise me you'll come?"

Without hesitation, I say, "I promise."

CHAPTER TWENTY-SEVEN

*T*he week goes by agonizingly slow, but things are mended with Jack. I receive texts morning, noon, and night from him, with cute messages, sexy pictures, or updates on the new restaurant. The sexy pictures are by far my favorite, and we spend most evenings teasing each other or having phone sex. I can't wait to get to him this weekend. I plan on showing him exactly what I need from him.

I'm dying to know what surprise he has for me and can't wait until tomorrow. The plan is to meet at his house, and he will take me to wherever we were going. I pack a weekend bag, figuring I will be staying with him and making up for lost time. When everything is packed and ready for tomorrow, I lay down and try to get a little sleep. He requested I come down for breakfast at the diner first, so I have an early morning start. My phone lights up with an incoming text.

Jack: *Goodnight, beautiful. I can't wait to see your smiling face in the morning. Be prepared for anything.*

Me: *Anything, huh? Promises, promises.*

I hit send, and snuggle down into my bed, dreaming of Jack.

TRAFFIC IS light and I make it to his house in just under an hour. When I pull into the driveway, I watch him jog out in bare feet, jeans, and a fitted t-shirt. He looks good enough to eat. He's grinning from ear to ear as he approaches my car and opens the door for me.

"You made good time. Are you hungry?"

"No traffic, and yes, I am." *Not for food though.* He takes my bag from the backseat and we head inside the house. It's just as I remember it, and images run through my head of the times we spent in the shower, on the patio, and in his bed. I smile and my cheeks flush.

He leans down and places his lips by my ear. "Stop thinking about it, dirty girl. I'm not gonna last as it is, and knowing you're thinking about the fun we've had isn't helping me. I promise, after I show you the surprise, I'll let you have me any way you want."

"*Any* way?"

His hot breath on my ear sends a shiver through my body. "*Any* way." He stands up straight, takes my bag to the bedroom, and returns moments later. "Come on, breakfast awaits."

We talk the whole way to the diner about everything and anything. I tell him about my job and how I've started applying for new ones. "It's not fun anymore. I don't want to sit in front of a computer all day and listen to people complain. I want to do more than that. I want to make people happy."

"You could always look for something down this way. I know of an apartment you could stay in, free of rent, or a house if you want..." He trails off.

"That's sweet, Jack. Thank you very much. If something opens up around here that I think would be suitable, I'll look at that option."

He pulls into a parking spot and gets out to open the door for me. He loops my arm through his, and we walk toward the diner, a smile on each of our faces. Ushering me through the door first, we see Steph, and her face lights up. She pulls me into a tight embrace and whispers, "I'm so happy to see you. He's been so lost without you." She pulls back, smiles at us, and leads us to a table.

After breakfast, we make our way back to the car. He opens the door for me and watches me as I settle into the seat.

"What's wrong? Do I have something on my face?" I wipe my mouth with my fingers, brushing off invisible crumbs.

"No, you look perfect. Since this is a surprise, though, I don't want you to see it until the last moment." He reaches into his back pocket and pulls out a black blindfold. He gives me a look, asking permission, and I close my eyes. After he ties it around my head, I adjust it so it's comfortable. I thought he was going to close the door, but moments later, I feel his lips press down on mine. He licks along the seam of my lips, and I open to him, allowing him to dip his tongue in. I reach up and tangle my fingers through his hair, pulling him closer to me.

Finally, he pulls back, both of us breathless and panting. "I think we need to use this more often. I like knowing you can't see what I'm going to do to you." I can hear the smile in his words, and then he closes the door.

We don't drive very far before he puts the car in park. I reach up to take the blindfold off, but he places his hands over mine. "Not yet. Let me help you get out of the car." I hear the door close and he comes to my side, helping me slide out and stand. He places his hands on my shoulders and moves me to where he wants. "Are you ready?"

I nod my head, not trusting my voice. He pulls the blindfold off and wraps his arms around my waist, resting his chin on my shoulder. Across the street is *Little Sweet Shoppe,* and it is open, with a line of customers out the door. I place my hand over my mouth and try to keep the tears at bay. "How?" It's the only word I manage to get past the lump in the throat.

"When I ran after you the day of the signing... Where did you go, by the way?"

"I ran up the stairs a few flights and hid so you couldn't get to me," I reply bashfully.

"Ah. Anyway, after I came back without being able to get to you, Oliver and I had a long discussion. I convinced him to subdivide the shops and leave a small amount to reopen *The Sweet Shoppe.* It's not as big as before, but the recipes are still the same. I hired Denise back, and we've been back in business for two days. I have the paperwork inside so I can add you as an owner of the store."

I whip my head to look at him in disbelief. "I'm going to be an owner?"

"As long as you want to be."

"Yes!" I jump and wrap my arms around his neck, pulling him in for another kiss. I break it too soon and he groans. "So, what's the most popular item on the menu? Éclairs?"

He shakes his head. "Sweet and Spicy Brownies. They're a hit and have been selling out almost every day."

"Just like us, a little sweet and a little spicy. Thank you, Jack. I love it. I love you."

"Will you move back to run the bakery? I'll help you with everything, and there is no pressure to move in with me. Only if you want to."

I press my fingers to his lips to quiet him, a simple yes falling from my lips.

ACKNOWLEDGMENTS

My husband, Dan- Thank you for pushing me to do this. I'm excited to see where this journey will lead me. You are one of the many people who helped push me in this direction, and I love you so much for it! Thank you for also putting up with all my crazy antics to get stories right. I know this isn't your favorite genre, but I appreciate you listening to my ideas and stories.

My friends and family- Thank you for supporting me, even though I kept it a secret for so long from most of you. I love having you on my side, supporting me anyway you can.

Michelle Windsor- Thank you for being willing to talk to me about your experiences and pushing me in the right direction. Publishing this book is scary, and not as easy as it looks, but you have been there every step of the way to help me as I need it. I'm forever in your debt! If you haven't read anything by her, they are a must. She is amazing!

To my editor, Kendra and cover designer, Amanda- Thank you so much for all your advice and work. I'm so happy with how everything turned out. You both helped me publish a *real* book that looks like it could be on the shelves at a bookstore! I never thought I'd have that.

To all the readers- You guys rock! Thank you for taking the time to read a story from a new indie author. I have a bunch of ideas running around in my head, and I'm hoping to release more stories you will enjoy.

Kendra's Editing and Book Services:
www.kendragaither.com

Amanda Walker PA and Design Services:
www.amandawalkerpa.com

ABOUT THE AUTHOR

Cara Wade is a daydreamer and a lifelong teenybopper. Boy bands forever! She would love to spend the day in the kitchen baking up sweet treats but hates doing the dishes after. When she is not writing (or suffering writer's block) you can find her reading, hiking, or relaxing by the water. She lives in northern Massachusetts with her loving husband.

 facebook.com/authorcarawade

 twitter.com/author_carawade

 instagram.com/authorcarawade

Made in the USA
Columbia, SC
21 September 2018